THE GREEN OVERCOAT

The Green Overcoat

BY

HILAIRE BELLOC

BOOKS FOR LIBRARIES PRESS

FREEPORT, NEW YORK

First published 1912
Copyright the Estate of the late H. Belloc.
Reprinted 1971 by arrangement with
A. D. Peters & Co.

INTERNATIONAL STANDARD BOOK NUMBER:
0-8369-5921-3

LIBRARY OF CONGRESS CATALOG CARD NUMBER:
70-165614

PRINTED IN THE UNITED STATES OF AMERICA

Dedicated to
MAURICE   BARING

I *

DEDICATION

My dear Maurice,

You wrote something called *The Green Elephant,*
and I have written something called *The Green
Overcoat.*

It is on this account that I dedicate to you my
work *The Green Overcoat,* although (and I take this
opportunity of reproaching you for the same) you
did not dedicate to me your work *The Green Elephant.*

An overcoat and an elephant have much in common, and also, alas! much in which they differ. An
elephant can be taken off, and so can an overcoat;
but, on the other hand, an overcoat can be put on,
and an elephant can not. I understand that
your elephant was not a real elephant; similarly
my overcoat is not a real overcoat, but only
an overcoat in a book. An overcoat is the largest
kind of garment, and an elephant is the largest kind
of beast, unless we admit the whale, which is larger
than the elephant, just as a dressing-gown is larger
than an overcoat; but this would lead me far!
Then, again, the elephant does not eat meat, or bite;
nor does an overcoat. He is most serviceable to
man; so is an overcoat. There are, however, rogue
elephants which are worse than useless, and give

less profit to their owner than if he had no elephant at all. The same is true of overcoats, notably of those which have got torn in the lining of the left armpit, so that the citizen on shoving his left arm therein gets it into a sort of *cul-de-sac,* which is French for blind-alley.

The elephant is expensive, so is the overcoat. The elephant is of a grave and settled expression, so is an overcoat. An overcoat hanging by itself upon a peg is a grave and sensible object, which in the words of the philosopher "neither laughs nor is the cause of laughter." So is an elephant encaged.

Again, man in conjunction with the elephant is ennobled by that conjunction, whether he ride upon its back or upon its neck or walk by its side, as does the keeper at the Zoo. The same is true of overcoats, which, whether we have them upon our backs or carry them over our arms, add something to our appearance. I could suggest many other points in common were this part of my work lucrative, and, as it were, in the business ; but it is not, and I must end. I might remind you that elephants probably grow old (though no man has lived to see it), that overcoats certainly do ; that elephants are of divers sex, and this is true also of the overcoat. On the other hand, an overcoat has no feet and it has two tails or none, whereas the elephant has four feet and but one tail, and that a very little one.

I must wind up by telling you why I have written of an " overcoat " and not a " greatcoat." " Great-coat " is the more vernacular ; " overcoat " I think

the more imperial. But that was not my reason.
I wrote " overcoat " because it was a word similar
in scansion and almost equivalent in stress-scheme
(wow !) to the word " elephant." Of course, if I
had considered length of syllable and vowel-value
it would have been another matter, for " elephant "
consists in three shorts, " overcoat " in a long, short
and long. The first is a what-you-may-call-'um,
and the second a thingumbob.

But I did not consider vowel sounds, and I was
indifferent to longs and shorts. My endeavour
was to copy you, and to have a title which would
get people mixed up, so that the great hordes of
cultivated men and women desiring to see your
play should talk by mistake of *The Green Overcoat.*

And then their aunts, or perhaps a prig-visitor,
would say : " Oh, no, that is the *book !* " In this
way the book would be boomed. That was my
game.

If people had done this sort of thing before it
would not work now ; but they haven't.

Now, Maurice, I end this preface, for I cannot
think of anything more to write.

H. BELLOC.

CONTENTS

x

CONTENTS

The Green Overcoat

CHAPTER I

In which the Green Overcoat takes a Journey

PROFESSOR HIGGINSON — to give him his true name—was a psychologist, celebrated throughout Europe, and recently attached to the modern and increasingly important University called the Guelph University, in the large manufacturing town of Ormeston. His stipend was £800 a year.

He was a tall, thin man, exceedingly shy and nervous, with weary, print-worn eyes, which nearly always looked a little pained, and were generally turned uneasily towards the ground. He did not dress carefully. He was not young. He had a trick of keeping both hands in his trouser pockets. He stooped somewhat at the shoulders, and wore a long, grey beard. He was a bachelor, naturally affectionate by disposition, but capable of savagery when provoked by terror. His feet were exceedingly large, and his mind was nearly always occupied by the subject which he professed.

This excellent man, in his ill-fitting evening suit,

13

had just said good-bye after an agonised party, upon Monday, the 2nd of May, at the house of Sir John Perkin, a local merchant of ample but ill-merited fortune.

It was as yet but midnight, the rooms were full, and he hoped to slip out early and almost unobserved.

Professor Higginson sidled aimlessly into the study that was doing duty as a cloakroom, sidled out again on remembering that he had not left his things there, and next turned to gaze almost as aimlessly at a series of pegs on which he hoped to find a familiar slouch hat, rather greasy, and an equally familiar grey Inverness which was like his skin to him. The slouch hat was there. The Inverness was gone.

Was it gone ? The Professor of Psychology was a learned man, and his sense of reality was not always exact. Had he come in that Inverness after all ? . . . The more he thought about it the less certain he was. He remembered that the May night, though very cold, had been fine as he came. He had no precise memory of taking off that Inverness or of hanging it up. He walked slowly, ruminating upon the great problem, towards the door of the hall ; he inwardly congratulated himself that there was no servant present, and that he could go through the dreadful ordeal of leaving the house without suffering the scrutiny of a human being. No carriage had yet drawn up. He opened the door, and was appalled to be met by a violent gust and a bitter, cold, driving rain.

Now the Professor of Psychology was, like the

domestic cat, of simple tastes, but he hated rain
even more than does that animal. It bitterly dis-
agreed with him, and worse still, the oddity of
walking through the streets in evening clothes
through a raging downpour, with a large expanse of
white shirt all drenched, was more than his nerves
could bear.

He was turning round irresolutely to seek once
again for that Inverness, which he was now more
confident than ever was not there, when the Devil,
who has great power in these affairs, presented to
his eyes, cast negligently over a chair, a GREEN
OVERCOAT of singular magnificence.

The green of it was a subdued, a warm and a
lovely green ; its cloth was soft and thick, pliable
and smooth ; the rich fur at the collar and cuffs was
a promise of luxury in the lining.

Now the Devil during all Professor Higginson's
life had had but trifling fun with him until
that memorable moment. The opportunity, as the
reader will soon discover, was (from the Devil's
point of view) remarkable and rare. More, far
more, than Professor Higginson's somewhat sterile
soul was involved in the issue.

The Green Overcoat appeared for a few seconds
seductive, then violently alluring, next—and in a
very few seconds—irresistible.

Professor Higginson shot a sin-laden and frightened
glance towards the light and the noise and the
music within. No one was in sight. Through the
open door of the rooms, whence the sound of the

party came loud and fairly drunken, he saw no face
turned his way. The hall itself was deserted. Then
he heard a hurl of wind, a dash of rain on the hall
window. With a rapidity worthy of a greater game,
and to him most unusual, he whisked the garment
from the chair, slipped into the shadow of the door,
struggled into the Green Overcoat with a wriggle
that seemed to him to last five weeks—it was, as a
fact, a conjuror's trick for smartness—and it was on !
The Devil saw to it that it fitted.

It was all right. He would pretend some mistake,
and send it back the *very first thing* next morning ;
nay, he would be an honest man, and send it back
at once by a messenger the moment he found out his
mistake on getting to his lodgings. So wealthy an
overcoat could only belong to a great man—a man
who would stay late, very late. Come, the Green
Overcoat would be back again in that house before
its owner had elected to move. He would be no
wiser ! There was no harm done, and he could not
walk as he was through the rain.

Alas ! These plausible arguments proceeded, had
the Professor but known it, from the Enemy of
Souls ! *He*, the fallen archangel, foresaw that
coming ruin to which his lanky and introspective
victim was unhappily blind. Dons are cheap meat
for Devils.

The door was shut upon the learned man. He
went striding out into the drenching storm, down
the drive towards the public road. And as he went
he carried a sense of wealth about him that was

very pleasurable in spite of the weather. He had never known such raiment !

His way down the road to his lodgings would be a matter of a mile or more. The rain was intolerable. He was wondering as he reached the gate whether there was any chance of a cab at such an hour, when he was overjoyed to hear the purring of a taxi coming slowly up behind him. He turned at once and hailed it. The taxi halted, and drew up a little in front of a street light, so that the driver's face was in shadow. He gave his address, opened the door and stooped to fold up his considerable stature into the vehicle.

He had hardly shut the door, and as he was doing so, felt, or thought he felt, some obstacle before him, when the engine was let out at full speed. The cab whirled suddenly round in the opposite direction from that which he had ordered, and as Professor Higginson was jolted back by the jerk into his seat, his left arm clutched at what was certainly a human form ; at the same moment his struggling *right* arm clutched *another*, crouched apparently in the corner of the cab.

He had just time to begin, " I beg your ——" when he felt each wrist held in a pair of strong hands and a shawl or cloth tightening about his mouth. All that he next attempted to say was lost to himself and to the world. He gave one vigorous kick with his long legs ; before he could give a second his feet were held as firmly as his hands, and he felt what must have been a handkerchief being tied

uncomfortably tightly round his ankles, while his
wrists were still held in a grasp that suggested something professional.

Professor Higginson's thoughts were drawn out
of their daily groove. His brain raced and pulsed,
then halted, and projected one clear decision—
which was to sit quite quiet and do nothing.

The driver's back showed a black square against
the lamp-lit rain. He heard, or would hear, nothing.
He paid no heed to the motions within, but steered
furiously through the storm. For ten good minutes
nothing changed.

The beating rain outside blurred the window-
panes, and the pace at which they drove forbade
the Philosopher any but the vaguest guesses at the
road and the whereabouts.

The public lights of the town had long since been
left behind ; rapid turns had begun to suggest
country lanes, when, after a sharper jolt than usual,
the machine curved warily through a gate into a
narrow way, the brakes were put on sharply, the
clutch was thrown out, and the cab stopped dead.
It was halted and its machine was panting down in
some garden, the poverty and neglect of which
glared under the acetylene lamps. The disordered,
weedy gravel of the place and its ragged laurels
stood out unnaturally, framed in the thick darkness.
The edge of the light just caught the faded brick
corner of an old house.

Professor Higginson had barely a second in which
to note a flight of four dirty stone steps leading to

a door in the shadow, when his captors spoke for the first time.

" Will you go quietly ? " said the one crouching before him—he that had tied his ankles.

The Professor assented through his gag with a voice like the distant lowing of a cow. The strong grip that held his wrists pulled his arms behind him, the taxi door was opened, and he was thrust out, still held by the hands. He poised himself upon his bound feet, and whoever it was that had spoken— he had a strong, young voice, and looked broad and powerful in the half-light behind the lamps— began unfastening the handkerchief at his ankles. Professor Higginson was not a soldier. He was of the Academies. He broke his parole.

The moment his feet were free he launched a vigorous kick at his releaser (who hardly dodged it), emitted through his gag a dull sound full of fury, and at the same instant found himself bumped violently upon the ground with his legs threshing the air in all directions. It was the gentleman who held his wrists behind him that was the author of this manœuvre, and even as he achieved it he piped out in a curious high voice that contrasted strangely with the strength he had just proved—

" Hit him, Jimmy ! Hit him in the face ! "

" Not yet," said Jimmy ominously. " Jerk him up, Melba ! "

At some expense to the Professor's nerves Melba obeyed, and the learned Pragmatist found himself once more upon his feet. He kicked out vigorously behind, but only met the air. It was as he had dreaded! He had to deal with professionals!

"All right, Jimmy?" came in a young, well-Englished and rather tired drawl from the driver.

The engine was still panting slightly.

"Yes, Charlie," said Jimmy cheerfully. "Off you go!"

"Good night," said the young, well-Englished and rather tired drawl again.

The clutch caught, the engine throbbed faster, the untidy gravel crunched under the motor as it turned a half circle to find the gate, and in doing so cast a moment of fierce light upon the stained and dirty door of the house.

The gagged victim noted that the door was open ; there had been preparation, and the signs of it did not reassure him.

His captor thrust him against that door, into the dark hall within. The other one, the one he had heard called "Jimmy" followed, shut the door, and struck a match.

There was revealed in the flare a passage between perfectly bare walls, dusty, uncarpeted floor boards, still bearing the faint marks of staining at their edges, a flight of stairs with flimsy bannisters, many of them broken—for the rest, nothingness.

"Melba" (if I may call that gentleman by the name his associates had given him) was busy at the Professor's wrists with something more business-like than a handkerchief. He was tying them up scientifically enough (and very tight) with a piece of box-cord.

Jimmy, opening the door of a room on the ground floor that gave into this deserted passage, lit a candle within. Mr. Higginson found himself pushed through that door on to a chair in the room beyond. A moment later he was bound to that chair, corded up in a manner uncomfortably secure to its rungs and back by his ankles, elbows and knees. It was Melba that did the deed. Jimmy, coming in after, turned the key in the door, and joined his companion. Then the pair of them stood gazing at their victim for a moment, and the Professor had his first opportunity in all that bewildering night of discovering what kind of beings he had to deal with.

Melba was a stout, rather pasty-faced young man, with fat cheeks and blue, protuberant eyes, not ill-natured. He had very light, straight hair, and his face in repose seemed to clothe itself with a half smile which was permanent. It was surprising that such a figure should have that strength of forearm which the Professor had unfortunately experienced. But there is no telling a man till he strips, and Melba, who might very well have been a young lounger of the French Boulevards, was, as a matter of fact, an oarsman of an English University. He rowed. It was his chief recreation. He also read French novels, and was a fair hand at writing mechanical verse. But that is by the way, nor could the Professor as yet guess anything of this. He glared at the youth over his gag and took him in.

Jimmy was quite another pair of shoes. He was tall also, but clean cut and very dark, with the black eyes and hair and fresh colouring of a Gael. No trace of his native accent remained with him. Indeed, he had been born south of the border, but his supple strength and the balance of his body were those of the mountains. He had race. Unlike his colleague, he looked as strong as he was. Jimmy, if you care to know it, did not row ; he swam and dived. He swam and dived with remarkable excellence, and was the champion, or whatever it is called, of some district or other of considerable size. He was also of the University that had nourished Melba —Cambridge.

These two young men, a little blown, and perhaps a little excited, but manfully concealing their emotions under a gentlemanly indifference, seated themselves on either side of a table with the Professor gagged and bound upon the chair before them. So seated, they watched their prey.

Melba slowly filled an enormous pipe from an enormous pouch, keeping his round, blue eyes fixed and ready for any movement upon the Professor's part.

Jimmy lit a black cigarette with some affectation, blew a cloud of thin, blue smoke, and addressed the prisoner—

" Before we come to business, Brassington," he said, " how will you behave if we ungag you ? "

An appreciative and pacifist lowing proceeded from the gag.

" That's all very well," broke in Melba in his falsetto, " last time you said that you broke your word ! "

" Wmmmmmm ! " replied the Professor, shaking his head in emphatic negation.

" Yes, but you did," continued Melba shrilly. " You tried to kick Jimmy, and you tried to kick me, too, after I dumped you."

Jimmy waved his hand at Melba, commanding silence.

" Look here, sir," he said, " we had to do it. We don't like it, and in a way we 're sorry ; but we *had* to."

The Professor recalled all that he had read of lunacy in its various forms (and that was a great deal more than was good for him), but he could see no trace of insanity in either of the two faces before him. If anything, the innocence of youth which they betrayed, coupled with an obviously strained and unnatural determination, was quite the other way.

Melba chimed in with his high voice again—

" And lucky you didn't get something worse ! "

" Don't, Melba ! " said Jimmy authoritatively.

He was evidently the moderate man of the two, the man of judgment, and instinctively the learned victim determined to lean upon him in whatever incongruous adventures might threaten.

" We *had* to do it," continued Jimmy, " because there wasn't any law. Mind you, we haven't done this without asking! But when there isn't any law you have to take the law into your own hands, haven't you, Melba?" he said, turning to his accomplice.

"Yes," piped Melba, "civil and criminal. He ought to have a lathering."

His blue, prominent eyes had a glare of ferocity in them, and Professor Higginson hated him in his heart.

Jimmy again assumed control.

"If there had been a law, sir, we'd have sued you. We are sorry" (this repetition a little pompously), "and we do not want to expose you. Personally," he added, flicking the ash from his cigarette and putting on the man-of-the-world, "I find it an ungrateful thing to constrain an older man. But it will all be over soon, and what is more, we will do it decently if you pay like a gentleman."

At the word "pay" Professor Higginson's inexperience of the world convinced him that he was in the hands of criminals. He had read in certain detective stories how criminals were not, as some imagined, men universally deprived of collars, clad in woollen caps and armed with bludgeons, nor without exception of the uncultivated classes. He could remember many cases (in fiction) of the gentleman-criminal, nay, of the precocious gentleman-criminal—and apparently these were of the tribe.

For the second time that evening he came to a rapid decision and determined to pay.

He had upon him thirty shillings in gold, it was a sovereign and half sovereign, in the right-hand waistcoat pocket of his evening clothes, and he thought he also had in the right-hand trousers pocket a few loose shillings and coppers. It was a great deal to sacrifice. For all he knew, it was compounding a felony ; but he would risk that. He would think of it as a rather high hotel bill— and he would be free ! He nodded his gagged head, mooed cheerfully, and looked acquiescent with his eyes.

" That 's right ! " said Jimmy, greatly relieved (for in his heart he had never dared hope for so easy a solution). " That 's right ! " and he sighed contentedly. " That 's right," he repeated for the third time. " We are really very sorry, sir ! But it 'll seem all right afterwards. When you have kept your side of the bargain we shall *certainly* keep ours." He said it courteously. " All we want is the money, and when we have the money and you are free, why, sir, I hope you will not grudge us what we have done."

So it was all going to end happily after all ? The Professor almost felt himself at liberty again, hurrying home through the night—hurrying anywhere at his free will, loosed from that accursed place, when Jimmy added—

" Of course, you will have to sign the letter ? "

CHAPTER II

In which a Philosopher wrestles with the Problem of Identity

THE Professor was in deeper water than ever. He had been called some name or other at the beginning of this conversation. What name he could not remember. What the friendlier of the two beasts meant by "a letter" he could not conceive until Jimmy, continuing, partly enlightened him.

"You will have to sign the brief note we have drafted here to accompany your payment. It's obvious."

Professor Higginson dimly guessed that he was wanted to safeguard them in some way against the consequences of his kidnapping. . . . Well, he had made up his mind, and he would not depart from it. He nodded again cheerfully enough, and his eyes were as acquiescent as ever.

Jimmy leaned forward, and in set tones of some gravity, said formally—

"We understand, this gentleman and I, that you acknowledge the payment due to us, and if we take off the—er—the impediment which we were compelled to put over your mouth, you will act up to your promise, and you will pay us?"

For the third time the Professor nodded vigorously.

" And you will sign the note ? "

He nodded even more vigorously once again.

" Very well," said Jimmy in the tone of a great arbitrator who has managed to settle matters without unpleasantness. " Melba, be good enough to untie your aunt's shawl, which for the moment prevents this gentleman from performing his promise by word of mouth.   "

Melba did as he was bid, jerking—as Mr. Higginson thought—the knot in the fabric rather ungently. He treasured it up against him.

The shawl was off, Melba was seated again, and Professor Higginson breathed the night air untainted by the savour of an ancient human garment, and an aunt's at that.

" I need not repeat all I have just been saying," said Jimmy, " but you must confirm it before we go further."

" I do," said the Professor, with a curiously successful affectation of cheerfulness for so untrained an actor. " Yes, certainly, gentlemen, I confirm it."

There was, if anything, a little precipitancy in his manner, as though he were eager to pay, as he most certainly was to get rid of those ropes round his arms and legs.

There was another thing bothering the Pragmatist. The Green Overcoat, which still wrapped him all about, was being woefully delayed. If the delay lasted much longer the owner might miss it

. . . and then, the tight cords at its elbows were doing it no good. They might actually be *marking* it. The thought made Professor Higginson very uncomfortable indeed. He had no idea whose it was, but it certainly belonged to someone of importance. . . . He wished he had never seen it.

He was not to be the last to wish that, but Hell is a hard taskmaster and the Professor was caught.

"We think," said Jimmy a little pompously, "at least, I think ——" (after glancing at Melba).

"I don't," said Melba.

"Well, *I* think," continued Jimmy, "and I think we ought to think, that you are doing the right thing, and, well, I like to tell you so."

The relations between Jimmy and his prisoner were getting almost cordial. He pushed the table so that that prisoner, when he was untied, should be able to write upon it. He put before him a type-written sheet of note-paper, an envelope, an ink-bottle, and a pen, which, with the exception of the benches on which he and his companion sat, the table and the chair, were all the furniture the place contained.

"And now, sir," added Jimmy, going behind the Psychologist and releasing his elbows, "now, sir" (here he wound the rope round the Professor's waist, secured it, and left his legs still tied to the chair rungs), "now, sir, perhaps we can come to business!"

Poor Mr. Higginson had never been so cramped in his life. He was far from young. The circulation in his lower arms had almost stopped. He brought them forward painfully and slowly and composed them upon the table, then his right hand slowly sought his waistcoat pocket, where reposed the sovereign and half-sovereign of his ransom.

"Of course," he began, intending to explain the smallness of the sum, for he could not but feel that it was very little gold for so considerable a circumstance of paper formalities and violence, "of course ——" when Jimmy interrupted him.

"I need not tell you the sum," said that youth rather coldly.

"Oh, no," twittered Melba, "he knows *that* well enough!" Then added, "G-r-r-r!" as in anger at a dog.

"Well—er—gentlemen, I confess"—began Mr. Higginson, hesitating.

"To be frank," said Jimmy rather sharply, "we all three know the sum perfectly well, and you perhaps, sir, with your business habits and your really peculiar ideas upon honour, best of all. It's two thousand pounds," he concluded calmly.

"*Two thousand pounds?*" shrieked the Professor.

"What did you expect?" broke in Melba an octave higher. "A bonus and a presentation gold watch?"

"Two thousand pounds!" repeated the bewildered Philosopher in a gasping undertone.

"Yes," rapped out Jimmy smartly, "two thousand pounds! . . . Really! After all that has passed ——"

"But," shouted the Professor wildly, saying the first words that came to him, "I haven't got such a

sum in the world.   I—I don't know what you
mean ? "

Jimmy's face took on a very severe and dreadful
expression.

" Mr. Brassington," he began in a slow and modulated tone.

" I 'm not Mr. Brassington, whoever Mr. Brassington may be," protested the unhappy victim, half
understanding the portentous error. " What on
earth do you take me for ? "

Jimmy by this time was in a mood to stand no
nonsense.

" Mr. Brassington," he said, " you broke your
word to us once this evening when you kicked out
at Melba, and that ought to have been a lesson to
me.   I was foolish enough to believe you when
you gave your word a second time.   I certainly
believed it when you gave it a third time after
we released you."   (It was a very partial release,
but no matter.)   " Now," said he, setting his
lips firmly, " if you try to shuffle out of the main
matter, I warn you it will be the worse for you, very
much the worse for you, indeed.   You will be good
enough to sign us a cheque for two thousand pounds,
and to sign the type-written acknowledgment in
front of you."

Men in bewilderment do foolish things even when
they are men of judgment, and Professor Higginson
certainly was not that.   His next words were fatal.

" Do you suppose I carry a cheque-book on me ? "
he roared.

"Melba," said Jimmy quietly, in the tones of a general officer commanding an orderly, " go through him."

The Professor having said a foolish word, followed it by a still more foolish action. He dived into the right-hand pocket of the Green Overcoat with a gesture purely instinctive. Melba was upon him like a fat hawk, almost wrenched his arm from its socket, and drew from that right-hand pocket a noble great cheque-book of a brilliant red, with a leather backing such as few cheque-books possess, and having printed on it in bold plutocratic characters—

" John Brassington, Esqr.,
' Lauderdale,'
Crampton Park, Ormeston."

Melba conveyed the cheque-book solemnly to Jimmy, and the two young men sat down again opposite their involuntary creditor, spreading it out open before them in an impressive manner.

" Mr. Brassington," said Jimmy, " what do I see here ? Everything that I should have expected from a man of your prominence in the business world and of your known careful habits. I see neatly written upon the fly-leaf, ' *Private Account,*' and the few counterfoils to the cheques already drawn carefully noted. I perceive," continued Jimmy, summing up boldly, " the sum of £50 marked ' self ' upon the second of this month. The object of your

munificence does not surprise me. Upon the next
counterfoil I see marked £173 10s. It is in settle-
ment of a bill—a garage bill. I am glad to see that
you recognise and pay *some* of your debts. The
third counterfoil," he said, peering more closely,
" relates to a cheque made out only yesterday. It
is for £5, and appears to have been sent to your son,
who, as you know, is our honoured friend."

" I protest . . . " interrupted Professor Higginson
loudly.

" At your peril ! " retorted Melba.

" You will do well, Mr. Brassington, to let me
finish what I have to say," continued Jimmy. " I
say your *son*, our honoured friend, as you know
well—only too well ! These three cheques are your
concern, not ours. No further cheque has been drawn,
and on the *fourth* cheque form, Mr. Brassington,
you will be good enough to sign your name. You
will make it out to James McAuley—a small c and
a big A, if you please ; an *ey*, not an a—in your
letters you did not do me the courtesy to spell my
name as I sign it. You will then hand me the
instrument, and I will settle with my friend."

At the words " my friend " he waved courteously
to Melba, gave a ridiculous little bow, which in his
youthful folly he imagined to be dignified.

The Professor sat stolidly and said nothing. His
thoughts hurried confusedly within him, and the
one that ran fastest was, " I am in a hole ! "

" I do assure you, gentlemen," he said at last,
" that there is some great mistake. I have no doubt

hat—that a Mr. Brassington owes you the money,
no doubt at all. And perhaps you were even justified
in the very strong steps you took to recover it.
I should be the last to blame you." (The liar!)
"*But as I am not Mr. Brassington*, but, if you
want to know, Professor Higginson, of the Guelph
University, I cannot oblige you."

When the Professor had thus delivered himself
there was a further silence, only interrupted by
Melba's addressing to him a very offensive epithet.
"Swine!" he said.

"Are we to understand, Mr. Brassington," said
Jimmy, when he had considered the matter, "that
after all that you have said you refuse to sign?
Did you imagine" (this with rising anger in his voice)
"that we would compromise for a smaller sum?"

"I tell you I am not Mr. Brassington!" answered
the Psychologist tartly.

"Oh!" returned Jimmy, now thoroughly aroused
and as naturally as could be, "and you aren't wearing Mr. Brassington's clothes, Brassington, are you?
And this isn't Mr. Brassington's cheque-book, is it,
Brassington? And you're not a confounded old
liar as well as a cursed puritanical thief? Now,
look here, if you don't sign now, you'll be kept here
till you *do*. You'll be locked up without food,
except just the bread and water to keep you alive ;
and if you trust to your absence being noticed, I
can tell you it won't be. We know all about that.
You were going to Belgium for a week, weren't you,
by the night train to London? You were taking no

luggage, because you were going to pick up a bag at your London office, as you always do on these business journeys. You were going on business, and I only hope the business will wait. Oh, we know all about it, Brassington! We have a clear week ahead of us, and you won't *only* get bread and water in that week; and I don't suppose anybody would bother if we made the week ten days."

I have already mentioned in the course of this painful narrative the name of the Infernal Power. My reader will be the less surprised to follow the process of Professor Higginson's mind in this terrible crux. He sat there internally collapsed and externally nothing very grand. His two masters, stern and immovable, watched him from beyond the table with its one candle. It was deep night. There was no sound save the lashing of the storm against the window-panes.

He first considered his dear home (which was a pair of rooms in a lodging in Tugela Street, quite close to his work). Then there came into his mind the prospect of sleepless nights in a bare room, of bread and water, and *worse*. . . .

What was " worse " ?

His resolution sank and sank. The process of his thought continued. The eyes of the two young men, hateful and determined, almost hypnotised him.

If the money of this ridiculous John Brassington whoever he might be, was there in his pocket, he would stand firm. He hoped he would stand firm. But after all, it was not money. It was only a bit of paper. He would be able to make the thing right. . . . He was very ignorant of such things, but he knew it took some little time to clear a cheque. . . . He remembered someone telling him that it took three days, and incidentally he grotesquely remembered the same authority telling him that every cheque cost the bank sevenpence. . . . The rope hurt damnably, and he was a man who could not bear to miss his sleep, it made him ill. . . . And he was feeling very ill already. He could carefully note the number of the cheque, anyhow. Yes, he could do that. He had this man Brassington's address. He had the name of the bank. It was on the cheques. He would have the courage to expose the whole business in the morning. He would stop that cheque. He clearly remembered the Senate of the University having made a mistake two years before, and how the cheque was stopped. . . . It was a perfectly easy business. . . . Of course, the actual signing of another man's name is an unpleasant thing for the fingers to do, but that is only nervousness—next door to superstition. One must be guided by reason. Ultimately it would do no harm at all, for the cheque would never be cleared.

Professor Higginson leant lovingly upon that word "cleared." It had a technical, salutary sound. It was his haven of refuge. Cheques had to go up to London, hadn't they? and to go to a place called a Clearing House ? He knew that much, though economics were not his department of learning. He knew that much, and he was rather proud of it—as Professors are of knowing something outside their beat.

While the Mystery of Evil was thus pressing its frontal assault on poor Professor Higginson's soul, that soul was suddenly attacked in flank by a brilliant thought : the cheque would enable him to trace his tormentors !

Come, that really was a brilliant thought ! He was prouder of himself than ever. He would be actually *aiding* justice if he signed ! The police could always track down someone where there was paper concerned. No one could escape the hands of British Law if he had once given himself away in a written document !

This flank attack of the Evil One determined the Philosopher. In a subdued voice he broke the long silence. He said—

" Give me the pen ! "

Jimmy solemnly dipped the pen in the ink and handed it to him, not releasing the cheque-book, but tearing out the cheque form for him to sign ; and as he did so the unseen Serpent smiled. In a hand as bold as he could assume Professor Higginson deliberately wrote at the bottom right-hand corner the fatal words " JOHN BRASSINGTON."

He was beginning to fill in the amount, when to his astonishment the cheque was snatched from his hands, while Jimmy thundered out—

"Do you suppose, sir, that you can deceive us in such a childish way as *that?* Does a man ever sign his cheque like a copybook?"

He glared at the signature.

"It's faked! That's no more your signature, Old Brassington, than it's mine!" he shouted. "That's how you write."

With the words he pulled a note from his pocket and tossed it to the unhappy man.

Melba made himself pleasant by an interjection— "What a vile old shuffler it is!" he said.

And Mr. Higginson saw written on the note, dated but a week before—

"James Macaulay, Esq.,

"Sir,

"I will have no further correspondence with you upon the matter.

"I am,

"Your obedient Servant,

"J. Brassington."

It was a strong, hard but rapid hand, the hand of a man who had done much clerk's work in his youth, It had certainly no resemblance to the signature which the Psychologist had appended to the cheque form, and that form now lay torn into twenty pieces by the angry Jimmy, who had also torn up the counterfoil and presented him with another cheque.

"I can't do it, gentlemen!" he said firmly—it was indeed too true—"I can't do it!"

2 *

Melba jumped up suddenly.

" I 'm not going to waste any more time with the old blighter ! " he said shrilly.   " Come on, Jimmy ! " and Jimmy yielded.

They blew out the candle, left the room with a curse, turning the key in the lock from the outside, and the unfortunate Mr. Higginson was left bound tightly to his chair in complete darkness, and I am sorry to say upon the verge of tears.

Nature had done what virtue could not do, and the Professor was stumped.

CHAPTER III

*In which the Green Overcoat appears as a point
of religion by not being there*

IN the smoking-room of Sir John Perkin's house
upon the same evening of Monday, the 2nd of May,
sat together in conversation a merchant and a friend
of his, no younger, a man whose name was Charles
Kirby, whose profession was that of a solicitor. The
name of the merchant who had retired apart to enjoy
with this friend a reasonable and useful conversation,
was Mr. John Brassington. He was wealthy, he
dealt in leather; he was a pillar of the town of
Ormeston, he had been its mayor. He was an
honest man, which is no less than to say the noblest
work of God.

Mr. John Brassington was, in this month of May,
sixty years of age. He was tall, but broad in shoulder
though not stout. He carried the square grey
whiskers of a forgotten period in social history.
He had inherited from his father, also a mayor of
Ormeston, that good business in the leather trade; it
was a business he had vastly increased. He had not
been guilty in the whole of his life of any act of mean-
ness or of treachery where a competitor was concerned,
nor of any act of harshness in the relations between

39

himself and any of his subordinates. His expression was in one way determined, in another rather troubled and uncertain ; by which I mean that there were strong lines round the mouth which displayed a habit of decision in business affairs, some power of self-control, and a well ordered life ; but his lips were mobile and betrayed not a little experience of suffering, to which we must attribute certain extremes which his friends thought amiable, but which his critics (for he had no enemies) detested.

Mr. Brassington had married at thirty-one years of age a woman quiet in demeanour, and in no way remarkable for any special talent or charm. She was the daughter of a clergyman in the town. She brought him a complete happiness lasting for four years. She bore him one child, and shortly after the birth of that child, a son, she died.

Now Mr. Brassington, like most of his kind, was a man of strong and secret emotions. He loved his country, he was attached to the pictures which the public press afforded him of his political leader, and he adored his wife. Her death was so sudden, the habit of his married life, though short, had struck so deep a root in him, that from the moment of losing her he changed inwardly and there began to appear in him those little exaggerations of which I have spoken. The best of these was too anxious an attachment to the son who must inherit his wealth. The next best a habit of giving rather too large and unexpected sums of money to objects which rather too suddenly struck him as worthy. To these habits of mind he added excursions into particular fields of morals. In one phase he had been a teetotaller. He escaped from this only to fall into the Anti-Foreign-Atrocities fever. He read Tolstoy for one year, and then passed from that emotion into a curious fit of land nationalisation. Finally, he settled down for good into the Anti-Gambling groove.

By the time this last spiritual adventure had befallen Mr. Brassington he was nearer fifty than forty years of age, and the detestation of games of hazard was to provide him for the rest of his life with such moral occupation as his temperament demanded.

Certain insignificant but marked idiosyncrasies in his dress accompanied this violence of moral emotion. For some reason best known to himself, he never carried an umbrella or a walking-stick. He wore driving gloves upon every possible occasion, suitable and unsuitable, and he affected in particular, in all weathers not intolerably warm, a remarkable type of Green Overcoat with which the reader is already sufficiently acquainted. The irreverent youth of his acquaintance had given it a number of nicknames, and had established a series in the lineage of this garment, for as each overcoat grew old it was regularly replaced by a new one of precisely the same cloth and dye, and lined with the same expensive fur.

He told not a soul—only his chief friend and (of course) his servants had divined it—but Mr. Brassington lent to that Green Overcoat such private

worship as the benighted give their gods. It was a
secret and strange foible. He gave to it in its
recurrent and successive births power of fortune and
misfortune. Without it, he would have dreaded
bankruptcy or disease. In the hands of others, he
thought it capable of carrying a curse.

The son to whom his affections were so deeply
devoted bore the three names of Algernon Sawby
Leonidas (Sawby had been his mother's family
name), and was now grown up to manhood. He had
been at Cambridge, had taken his degree the year
before, but had lingered off and on for his rowing,
and "kept his fifth year." He divided his time
between London lodgings and the last requirements
of his college.

On that day in May with which I am dealing
it was to consult upon this son of his that Mr.
Brassington had left the crowd at Sir John Perkin's
and had shut himself with Charles Kirby into the
smoking-room.

Mr. Kirby was listening, for the fifteenth or
twentieth time, to his friend's views upon Algernon
Sawby Leonidas, which lad, in distant Cambridge,
was at that moment doing precisely what his father
and his father's lawyer were about, drinking port,
but with no such long and honest life behind him as
theirs.

It was Mr. Kirby's way to listen to anything his
friends might have to say—it relieved them and
did not hurt him. In the ordinary way he cared
nothing whether he was hearing a friend's tale for

the first or for the hundredth time ; he had no nerves
where friendship was concerned, and friendship was
his hobby.   But in this late evening he did feel a
movement of irritation at hearing once again in full
detail the plans for Algernon's life spun out in their
regular order, as though they were matter for novel
advice.

Mr. Brassington was at it again—the old, familiar
story ! How, properly speaking, the Queen should
have knighted him when she came to Ormeston
during his mayoralty ; how, anyhow, King Edward
might have given him a baronetcy, considering all
he had done during the war.   How he didn't want it
for himself, but he thought it would steady his son.
Now he would have nothing to do with paying for
such things ; how he had heard that the usual price
was £25,000 ; how that was robbing his son ! Robbing his son, sir ! Robbing his son of a thousand
pounds a year, sir ! How Mr. Brassington would
have that baronetcy given him for the sake of his
son, of hearty goodwill, or not at all.

Mr. Kirby listened, more and more bored.

" I 've told you, Brassington, twenty times !
They came to me about it and you lost your temper.
They came to me about it again the other day, and
it 's yours for the asking, only, hang it all ! you must
do *something* public again, they must have a peg to
hang it on."

Whereat Mr. Kirby's closest and oldest friend
went at him again, recited the baronetcy grievance
at full length once more, and concluded once

more with his views upon Algernon Sawby Leonidas.

When Mr. Brassington had come to the end of a sentence and made something of a pause, Mr. Kirby said—

" I thought you were going to Belgium ? "

Mr. Brassington was a little pained.

" I have arranged to take the night mail," he said gravely. " I shall walk down. Will you come to the station with me ? "

" Oh, yes ! " said Mr. Kirby briskly. " It 'll give me a nice walk back again all through the rain. If you think all that about Algernon you shouldn't have sent him to Cambridge."

" I sent him to Cambridge by your advice, Kirby," said Mr. Brassington with dignity.

" I would give it again," said Mr. Kirby, crossing his legs. " It 's an extraordinary thing that a rich man like Perkin has good port one day and bad port another. . . . He ought to go to Cambridge. I have a theory that everyone should go to Cambridge who can afford it, south-east of a line drawn from —— "

" Don't, Charles, don't," said Mr. Brassington, a little pained, " it 's very serious ! "

Mr. Kirby looked more chirpy than ever.

" I didn't say your ideas were right ; I don't think they are. I said that if you had those ideas it was nonsense to send him to Cambridge. Why shouldn't he drink ? Why shouldn't he gamble ? What 's the harm ? "

"What 's the —— ? " began John Brassington, with a flash in his eyes.

"Well, well," said Kirby soothingly, " I don't say it 's the best thing in the world. What I mean is you emphasise too much. You know you do. Anyhow, John, it doesn't much matter ; it 'll all come right."

He stared at the fire, then added—

"Now, why can't I get coals to burn like that ? Nothing but pure white ash ! "

He leant forward with a grunt, stirred the fire deliberately, and watched the ash with admiration as it fell.

"Kirby," said John Brassington, "it will break my heart ! "

"No it won't ! " said Mr. Kirby cheerfully.

"I tell you it *will !* " replied the other with irritation, as though the breaking of the heart were an exasperating matter. "And one thing I am determined on—determined —— " The merchant hesitated, and then broke out abruptly in a loud voice, "Do you know that I have paid his gambling debts four times regularly ? Regularly with every summer term ? "

"It does you honour, John," said Mr. Kirby.

"Ah, then," said Mr. Brassington, with a sudden curious mixture of cunning and firmness in his voice, "I haven't paid the last, though ! "

"Oh, you haven't ? " said Mr. Kirby, looking up. He smelt complications.

"No, I haven't . . . ! I gave him fair warning,"

said the elderly merchant, setting his mouth as
squarely as possible, but almost sobbing in his heart.
" Besides which it 's ruinous."

" I wonder if he gave the young bloods fair
warning ? " mused Mr. Kirby. " Last Grand
National —— "

" Oh, Lord, Charles ! " burst out Mr. Brassington,
uncontrollable. " D'ye know what, what that cub
shot me for ? Curse it all, Kirby, two thousand
pounds ! "

" The devil ! " said Charles Kirby.

" It is the Devil," said John Brassington em-
phatically.

And it was, though he little knew it, for it was in
that very moment that the Enemy of Mankind was
at work outside in the hall upon the easy material
of Professor Higginson. It was in that very moment
that the Green Overcoat was enclosing the body of
the Philosopher, and was setting out on its adventures
from Sir John Perkin's roof. Even as Mr. Brassingon
spoke these words the outer door slammed. Kirby,
looking up, suddenly said—

" I say, they 're going ! What about your train ? "

" There 's plenty of time," said Brassington
wearily, " it 's only twelve. Do listen to what I am
saying."

" I 'm listening," said Kirby respectfully.

" Well," went on Mr. Brassington, " there 's the
long and the short of it, I won't pay."

Mr. Kirby poked the fire.

" The thing to do," he said at last in a meditative

sort of tone, " is to go down and give the young cubs Hell ! "

" I don't understand you, Charles," said Mr. Brassington quietly ; " I simply don't understand you. I was written to, and I hope I replied with dignity. I was written to again, and I answered in a final manner. I will not pay."

" I have no doubt you did," said Mr. Kirby. " It 's a curious thing how eagerly a young man will take to expectations ! "

" You simply don't know what you 're saying, Charles," answered Mr. Brassington ; " and if I didn't know you as well as I do, I 'd walk out of the room."

" I know what I am saying exactly," riposted Mr. Kirby with as much heat as his quizzical countenance would allow. " I was going to follow it up if you hadn't interrupted me. I say it 's a curious thing how a young man will be moved by expectations. That 's why they gamble. Thank God, I never married ! They like to see something and work for it. That 's why they gamble. You won't understand me, John," he said, putting up a hand to save an interruption ; " but that 's why when I was a boy my father put me into the office and said that if I worked hard something or other would happen, something general and vague — esteem, good conscience, or some footling thing called success."

" I wish you wouldn't say ' footling,' " interjected John Brassington gravely.

" I didn't," answered Mr. Kirby without changing

a muscle, "it's a horrible word. Anyhow, if my dad had said to me, ' Charles, my boy, there's £100 for you in March if you keep hours, but if you're late *once* not a farthing,' by God, John, I'd have worked like a nigger ! "

Mr. Brassington looked at the fire and thought, without much result.

" I can't pay it, Charles, and I won't," he said at last. " I've said I wouldn't, and that's enough. I have written and said I wouldn't, and that's more. But even if I had said nothing ' and had written nothing, I wouldn't pay. He must learn his lesson."

" Oh, he'll learn that all right ! " said Mr. Kirby carelessly. " He's learning it now like the devil. It's an abominable shame, mind you, and I don't mind telling you so. I've a good mind to send him the money myself."

" If you do, Charles," said John Brassington, with one of his fierce looks, " I'll, I'll —— "

" Yes, that's what I was afraid of," said Mr. Kirby thoughtfully. " You're an exceedingly difficult man to deal with. . . . I shouldn't have charged him more than five per cent. You'll lose your train, John."

John Brassington looked at his watch again.

" You haven't been much use to me, Charles," he said, sighing as he rose.

" Yes, I have, John," said Mr. Kirby, rising in his turn. " What do you do with your evening clothes when you run up to town by the night train like this ? "

"I change at my rooms in town when I get in, Charles," said Mr. Brassington severely, "you know that as well as I do—and I wear my coat up to town."

"They say you wear it in bed," was Mr. Kirby's genial answer. "I'll come out and help you on with it, and we'll start."

The two men came out from the smoking room into the hall. They found a number of guests crowding for their cloaks and hats. They heard the noise of wheels upon the drive outside.

"I told you how it would be, John," said Mr. Kirby. "You won't be able to get through that crush. You won't get your coat in time, and you'll miss the train."

"That's where you're wrong, Charles," said Mr. Brassington, with a look of infinite organising power. "I always leave my coat in the same one place in every house I know."

He made directly for the door, where a large and sleepy servant was mounting guard, stumbled to a peg that stood in the entry, and discovered that the coat was gone.

There followed a very curious scene.

The entry was somewhat dark. It was only lit rom the hall beyond. Mr. Kirby, looking at his friend as that friend turned round from noting his loss, was astonished to see his face white—so white that it seemed too clearly visible in the dark corner, and it was filled with a mixture of sudden fear and

sudden anger. From that face came a low cry
rather than a phrase—

"It 's gone, Charles!"

The louty servant started. Luckily none of the
guests heard. Mr. Kirby moved up quickly and put
his hand on Brassington's arm.

"Now, do manage yourself, John," he said.
"What 's gone?"

"My Green Overcoat!" gasped Mr. Brassington
in the same low tone passionately.

"Well?"

"Well! You say 'well'—you don't understand!"

"Yes, I do, John," said Mr. Kirby, with a sort of
tenderness in his voice. "I understand perfectly.
Come back here with me. Be sensible."

"I won't stir!" said Mr. Brassington irresolutely.

Mr. Kirby put a hand affectionately upon his old
friend's shoulder and pushed him to the door of the
smoking-room they had just left. He shut that
door behind him. None of the guests had noticed.
It was so much to the good.

"It 's gone! It 's gone!" said John Brassington
twice.

He had his hands together and was interlacing the
fingers of them nervously.

Mr. Kirby was paying no attention; he was
squatting on his hams at a sideboard, and saying—

"It 's lucky that I do John Perkin's business for
him, I 'm being damned familiar."

He brought out a decanter of brandy, chucked

the heel of Mr. Brassington's port into the fire, and
poured out a glassful of the spirit.

"I always forget your last craze, John," he said;
"but if I was a doctor I should tell you to drink
that."

John Brassington drank a little of the brandy, and
Mr. Kirby went on—

"Don't bother about Belgium to-night, my boy.
In the first place, take my overcoat. I am cleverer
than you in these crushes, I don't even hang it on
a peg. I leave it" (and here he reached behind
a curtain), " I leave it here," and he pulled it
out.

It was no more than an easy mackintosh without
arms. He put it on his unresisting friend, who simply
said—

"What are you going to do, Charles?"

"I am going to take orders," said Charles Kirby,
suddenly pulling out from his pocket a square of
fine, black silk, and neatly adjusting it over his shirt
front. "I haven't got a parson's dog collar on, but a
man can walk the streets in this. After all, some of
the clergy still wear the old-fashioned collars and
white tie. don't they?"

John Brassington smiled palely.

"Oh, it's in the house!" he said. "It's sure to
be in the house somewhere!"

"Now, John," said Charles Kirby firmly, "don't
make a fool of yourself. *Don't ask for that coat.*
It's the one way not to get it. Stay where you are,
and I'll bring you news."

He went out, and in five minutes he came back with news.

"Fifty people went out before we got up, John. No one knows who they were. The idiot at the door could only remember the Quaker lot and My-lord, and Perkin's so fussed that he can do nothing but swear, and that's no use. You've simply got to come along with me, and we'll walk home through the rain. Take Belgium at your leisure."

"It isn't Belgium that's worrying me!" said poor Mr. Brassington.

"No, *I* know," said Charles Kirby soothingly. "*I* understand."

The two men went out into the night and the storm. Charles Kirby enjoyed bad weather; it was part of his manifold perversity. He tried to whistle in the teeth of the wind as they went along the main road towards the Crampton Park suburb of the town. Brassington strode at his side.

"You didn't order a carriage," said Kirby after a little while; "you didn't know it was going to rain. I suppose that Green Overcoat of yours has got luck in the lining?"

"It has a cheque-book of mine in the pocket," said John Brassington.

"Yes, but that's not what you're bothering about," said Mr. Kirby. "You're bothering about the luck. For a man who hates cards, John, you're superstitious."

For some paces Brassington said nothing, then he said—

"Long habit affects men."

"Of course it does," said Mr. Kirby, with the fullest sympathy. "That is why so many people are afraid of death. They're afraid of the change of habit."

And after that nothing more was said until they came to the lodge gates of that very large, ugly, convenient and modern house, which John Brassington had built and for no reason at all had called "Lauderdale."

"Shall I come up to the door with you, John?" said Mr. Kirby.

"If you don't mind," answered Brassington doubtfully.

"Not a bit," said Mr. Kirby cheerfully. "If I had grounds as big as yours I shouldn't go through them alone."

The two men walked up the short way to the main door. When it was opened for them, the first thing Mr. Brassington said to his servant was—

"Has anyone brought back my overcoat?"

The servant had seen nothing of it.

"It's not here," said Mr. Brassington, turning round to Mr. Kirby. "Come in."

"No, I won't, John," said Mr. Kirby. "I'll ring you up in the morning. I'll do better than come in, I'll try and find it for you."

"You're a good friend, Charles," said John Brassington, with meaning and simplicity. He had got a blow.

"Meanwhile, John," said Kirby, standing outside

and dripping in the rain, " remember it 's doing some other fellow heaps of good. Heaps and heaps and heaps ! I should like a drink."

" Come in," said Brassington again.

" Very well," said Kirby as he came in ; " but I won't take off my hat."

Mr. Brassington had wine sent for, and Charles Kirby drank.

" It 's too late to drink wine," he said when he had taken three or four glasses. " It 's a good thing that I don't care about the office, isn't it ? Good night."

The servant held the door open for him, and Brassington walked off ; but when the master of the house was out of sight and hearing, Mr. Kirby stopped abruptly on the steps, and turning to the servant just before the door was shut upon him, said—

" Who did you speak to to-day about your master's overcoat ? "

The man was so startled that he blurted out—

" Lord, sir, I never said a word ! It was the coach-man who spoke to the young gentleman when the young gentleman saw it. He didn't borrow it, sir. He was a friend of Mr. Algernon's."

" Was he ? " said Mr. Kirby. " Well, all right," and he turned to go down the drive. He reflected that it was a mile and a half to his own home ; but then, there was the storm still raging and he liked it, and, thank Heaven, he never got up earlier than he could help. He therefore proceeded to whistle, and as he whistled, to consider curiously the soul of that old friend of thirty years, whom he loved with all his heart. Next he made a picture of a young gentleman, a friend of his friend's son, coming and asking to see the Green Overcoat, and learning it by heart. Why? Mr. Kirby didn't know. He stacked the fact up on a shelf and left it there.

CHAPTER IV

*In which it is seen that University training fits
one for a business career*

THE dawn in the month of May comes much earlier
than most well-to-do people imagine. It comes
earlier than most people of the class which buys and
reads novels know, and as by this time I can be quite
certain that the reader has either bought, hired,
borrowed, or stolen this enchanting tale, I feel safe
in twitting him or her or it upon their ignorance.

The dawn in May comes so incredibly early that
the man who makes anything of a night of it is not
sleepy until broad daylight. Now, even those who
have formed but a superficial acquaintance with the
adventures of Professor Higginson will admit that
he had made a night of it. Such a night as even the
sacred height of Montmartre and the great trans-
pontine world of London hardly know. Providence
had not left him long to curse and despair in darkness bound to his chair. He was already exhausted,
but he could still think and act, when he perceived
that a sickly light was filling the room. So dawned
upon him Tuesday, the third of May, a date of
dreadful import for his soul.

It was then that the Psychologist remembered
that his arms were free.

In that wide reading of his to which I have several
times alluded, and which replaced for him the
coarser experiences of life, Professor Higginson had
learned of Empire Builders and strong men who
with no instrument but their good Saxon teeth had
severed the most dreadful fetters. How then should
he fail, whose two hands were at liberty, to divest
himself of his mere hempen bonds ?

He cursed himself for a fool—in modulated internal
language—for not having thought of the thing before.

He first surveyed all that his eyes could gather.
The box cord surrounded the Green Overcoat with a
sevenfold stricture. It was continuous. It curled
round the rungs and the legs of the chair, it tightly
grasped his ankles and his knees. Somewhere or
other it was knotted, and he must find that knot.

Heaven, or (as the Professor preferred to believe)
Development has given to the human arm and hand
an astonishing latitude and choice of movement.
Since the knot wasn't in sight, it must be behind him.
He felt gingerly along the cord with either hand, so
far as either hand would reach, but found it not.

He next decided that the knot must be beneath
him. The chair had wide arms, to which his body
was strictly bound. He bent as far as he could first
to one side and then to the other, but he could
discover no knot upon the seat beneath.

Once more he leant backwards (at some considerable expense of pain), and with the extreme tip of
his right middle finger just managed to touch a
lower rung at the back of the chair ; there at last he

found the accursed tangle. There he could tickle the outer edge of the damnable nexus of rope. There was the knot! Just out of reach!

In one strenuous and manly attempt to add one inch to his reach in that direction, he toppled the chair backwards and fell, striking the back of his head heavily against the floor.

The Professor was not pleased. He was horribly hurt, and for a moment he lay believing that all things had come to an end. But human instinct, fertile in resource, awoke in him. He swung his head and shoulders upwards spasmodically in a desperate effort to redress himself. Finding that useless, he deliberately turned over on his side, from this on to his knees, and so upon all fours, with the chair still tightly bound to him and riding him like a castle.

Having attained that honourable position—which is by all the dogmas of all the Universities the original attitude of our remote ancestors—he made a discovery.

In this native posture he was capable of progression, of progression with the chair burdening his back like the shell of a tortoise, and with his legs dragged numbly after him, but still of progression, for he could put one hand before the other after the fashion of a wounded bear, and so drag the remainder of his person in their wake.

In this fashion, as the light gradually broadened on the filthy and deserted apartment, Professor Higginson began an odyssey painful and slow all over the floor of his prison. He inspected its utmost corners in search of something sharp wherewith to cut the cord, but nothing sharp was to be found.

It was broad daylight by the time he had completed his circumnavigation and detailed survey. In the half light he had. hoped that the window might give upon the garden ; now that everything was fully revealed by the dawn, he was disappointed. The one window, as he cricked his neck to look up at it, gave upon nothing better than the brick wall of a narrow, dirty backyard. He slowly retraced his steps, or rather spoor, to the position he had originally occupied, and then with infinite labour, grabbing at the edge and legs of the table, he tilted the chair right side uppermost, and resumed the position of Man Enthroned.

He was exhausted.

He was exhausted ; but the new day always brings some kind of vigour in its train, and the Professor began once more to think and to determine, though the soul within him was a wet rag and his *morale* wholly gone. He was angry, so far as a man can be properly angry when weakened by such extremes of ill. He hated now not only those two young men, but all men. He would be free. He had a right to freedom. He would recover his own freedom by whatever means, and when he had recovered t, then he would do dreadful deeds !

There was no sound in the great lonely house. The rain outside had ceased. The ridiculous birds, grossly ignorant of his sorrows, were skreedling for

dear life like ungreased cartwheels. It was a
moment when wickedness has power, and oh!
Professor Higginson, with firmer face than ever he
had yet set, made up his mind to be free. . . . Once
free, he would undo all ill and wreak his vengeance.

He first took up from the table that note signed
John Brassington in strong, swift English writing.
He scanned it long and well.

He next took up the cheque form that had been
left him ; he lifted it with a gesture of purpose too
deliberate for such a character as his, and one that
nothing but the most severe fortune could have bred
in it.

He felt in a pocket for a bit of pencil, and then—
this time not on all fours, but dragging himself round
the edges of the table and the burden of the chair
along with him—he made for the window.

The angels and the demons saw Professor Higginson
do this dreadful thing ! He put against the lowest
pane (which he could well reach) the signed note of
John Brassington. The pure light of heaven's day
shone through it clear. He held firmly above it
with one of his free hands the bottom left-hand
corner of the cheque form, and he traced, Professor
Higginson traced, he traced lightly and carefully with
the pencil, he traced with cunning, with care, and with
skill the " J "—and the " o "—and the " h "—and the
" n," and the capital " B "—and the " r "—and the
" a "—and the " s "—and all the rest of the business !

The Good Angels flew in despair to their own
abode, leaving for the moment the luckless race of

men. The Bad Ones, as I believe, crowded the
room to suffocation ; but to use mere mortal terms,
Professor Higginson was alone with his wicked
deed.

It was too late to retrace his steps. He had
hardened his heart. With a series of ungainly
hops, aided by the edge of the table, he regained the
inkpot and the pen, and covered with a perfection
surely unnatural the pencil tracing he had made.
Professor Higginson had forged !

It would all come right. There was the " clearing " . . . and the thing called " stopping a
cheque," and anyhow—damn it, or rather dash it,
a man was of no use for a good cause until he was
free. . . . Yes, he had done right. He must
be free first. . . . Free, in spite of the bonds
which cut him as he leant half forward, half sideways,
with his eyes closed and his hands dropping on the
arms of the chair . . . free to take good deep
breaths . . . regular breaths, rather louder ones
he thought—then, as men on active service go to
sleep in the saddle, and sailors sleep standing at the
helm from fatigue, so, bound and cramped, the
Professor of Psychology and Specialist in Subliminal
Consciousness in the Guelph University of Ormeston,
England, slept.

When Professor Higginson awoke the birds had
ceased their song and had gone off stealing food.
The air was warm. A bright sun was shining upon
the wall of the dirty courtyard. He pulled out his
watch. It was a quarter to nine. He felt at once

3

reposed and more acutely uncomfortable, fresher and yet more in pain from the bonds round his legs and middle, and less friendly with the hard chair that had been his shell and was now his unwanted seat. As he looked at the watch, he remembered having broken the glass of it sometime ago. He remembered a splinter of that glass running into his hand, and—marvellous creative influence of necessity even in the academic soul!—he remembered that glass could cut.

He felt like a Columbus. He wished he could patent such things. He began gingerly to lift the glass from the case of his watch. It broke, and I am sorry to say did what it had done before—it ran into his finger. He sucked the wound, but was willing to forget it in his new-found key to delivery. With a small fragment of the splintered thing he began very painfully sawing at a section of the rope that bound him. He might as well have tried to cut down a fifteen-year oak with a penknife. All things can be accomplished with labour at last, but the life of man is a flash.

He looked desperately at the window, and another dazzling conception struck him. Surely his brain was burgeoning under the heat of nourishing adversity! It occurred to him to break a window-pane !

He did so. The glass fell outward and crashed on the courtyard below. With desperate courage but infinite precautions, he pulled at a jagged piece that remained. Here was something much more

like a knife! Triumphantly he began to saw away
at the cords, and to his infinite relief the instrument
made a rapid and increasing impression. A few
seconds more at the most, and he would have severed
the section. He would have two ends, and then, as
his new-born cunning told him, he had but to follow
up and unroll them and he would be free. But just
as the last strand was ready to give, as the biceps
muscle of his arm was only just beginning to ache
from the steady back and forth of his hand, he heard
hateful voices upon the stairs, the loud trampling
of four young and hardy booted feet upon the
uncarpeted wood, the key turned in the lock,
and Jimmy and Melba, if I may still so call them,
occupied the entry.

With nervous and desperate fingers Professor
Higginson was loosening as best he might the tangle
of his now severed bonds, when they were upon him,
and I greatly regret to say that the higher voiced of
the two young men was guilty of the common-place
phrase, "Ah! you would, would you?" accompanied by a sudden forced locking of the elbows
behind, which, bitterly offensive as it was, had
come to be almost as stale as it was offensive to the
Pragmatist of uelph University.

Even to Melba the Professor seemed a different
man from the victim of a few hours before. He
turned round savagely. He positively bit. In his
wrath he said—

"Let me go, you young devil!"

Mr. James McAuley in that same scurried

moment had seen and picked up the cheque. He echoed in graver tone—

"Let him go, Melba, don't be a fool! Mr. Brassington," he added, " you would really have been wiser to have done this last night. We had no intention to put any indignity upon you, but you know we had a right to our money. After all, we warned you. . . ."

Then, seeing the typewritten sheet unsigned, he said—

" It 's no good to us without this, Mr. Brassington."

Mr. Higginson, lowering and furtive like a caged cheetah, snarled and pulled the paper towards him. It was stamped with the business heading of the Brassington firm. It was brief and to the point :

" James McAuley, Esq.

" Dear Sir,

" After consultation with those best fitted to advise me, I have decided, though I still regard the necessity placed upon me as a grievous injustice, to liquidate my son's foolish debt.

" I enclose my cheque for £2,000, for which you will be good enough to send me a receipt in due form, and I am,

" Your obedient servant,

Then came the blank for signature. Professor Higginson with a very ugly face, uglier for his hours of torture, turned on the young men.

"I am to sign that, am I?"

"If you please, Mr. Brassington," said Jimmy, unperturbed.

"Well, then, I'll thank you to leave the room, you young fool, and your friend with you."

Melba and Jimmy looked at each other doubtfully.

"I cannot, will not do it," barked the wretched scientist, "if you stay here."

"After all, Mr. Brassington, we had all this out last night ——"

"Yes, and I wouldn't do it until you were gone, would I?" said Professor Higginson, scoring a point.

"After all, he can't do anything through that window, Melba, can he? Let's come out and wait. But I warn you, sir," he added, turning to the fallen man, "we shall hear all that you do, and we shall stop immediately outside the door."

"Go to Hell!" said Professor Higginson, using the phrase for the second time in his life, and after an interval of not less than twenty-three years.

Whereupon the young men retired, and the now hardened soul proceeded once again to trace, to pencil, and to sign.

"It's ready!" he shouted to the door as his pen left the paper.

His tormentors re-entered and possessed themselves of the document, and then, though Melba remained an enemy, Jimmy's demeanour changed.

"Mr. Brassington," he said, "we are very much obliged to you, very much obliged, indeed."

"So you ought to be," said Professor Higginson suddenly.

"Henceforward I beg you will regard these premises as your own," said Jimmy.

With these words he suddenly caught the Professor down upon the chair, took that chair upon one side, Melba took it upon the other, and they held and carried the unfortunate man rapidly through the open door, up three flights of uncarpeted stairs, until, assuring him of the honesty of their intentions, they deposited him upon a landing opposite a comfortable-looking green baize door. Then they stood to recover their breath, still holding him tightly upon either side, while ·Jimmy as spokesman repeatedly assured him that they meant him no ill.

"It's nothing but a necessary precaution, Mr. Brassington, we do assure you," he puffed. "You see, the cheque must be cleared. Not that we doubt your honour for a moment! You'll find all you want in there. You can untie yourself now that you've cut the rope, you know, and there's everything a man can possibly want. It's a solemn matter of honour between us, Mr. Brassington, that we'll let you out the *moment* the cheque's cleared. And there's plenty of food and good wine, Mr. Brassington, really good wine——"

"And ginger-ale, if you like the slops," added Melba; "a man like you would."

"We are very sorry," said Jimmy, by way of palliating the insult, "but you must see as well as

we do that it has to be done. Not that we doubt
your honour! Not for a moment!"

With these words he gave some mysterious signal
to Melba. The baize door was swung open and a
large oaken door within it was unbolted ; the chair
and the wretched man upon it were run rapidly
through, the bolt shot, and Jimmy, standing outside, asked, as in duty bound—

"You're not hurt? You're all right?"

A hearty oath assured him that all was well. He
tramped with his companion down the stairs, and
Mr. Higginson was again a prisoner and alone.

CHAPTER V

*In which Solitude is unable to discover the charms
which Sages have seen in her face*

THE Philosopher cursed gently, and then listened.

The steps of his tormentors grew fainter as they
reached the lower part of the house. Then he
heard, or thought he heard, the distant crunching
of boots on gravel. After that came a complete
silence.

It occurred to the ill-used gentleman that he was
free. He pulled savagely at the loose cords : got one
leg to move and then the other ; gradually unrolled
the cord and attempted to stand.

At first he could not. Nine hours of such confinement had numbed him. He felt also an acute pain,
which luckily did not last long, where his circulation
had been partially arrested at the ankles. In a few
minutes he could stand up and walk. It was then
that he began to observe his new surroundings.

He found himself in a large and very high room,
with a steep-pitched roof, soaring and sombre, quite
twenty feet above him. The walls were bare of
ornament, but still covered with a rich dark red
paper, darker, cleaner patches on which marked

places where pictures had hung. On the height of the roof, looking north, was a large skylight which lit the whole apartment. There was a good writing-table with pigeon-holes and two rows of drawers on either side. Upon this writing table stood a little kettle, a spirit stove, a bottle of methylated spirit, a tin of milk cocoa, three large loaves, a chicken, tinned meats, a box of biscuits, and, what was not at all to be despised, an excellent piece of Old Stilton Cheese. The thoughtful provider of these had even added a salt-cellar full of salt. There stood also upon the floor beside these provisions a large stone jar, which upon uncorking and smelling it he discovered to contain sherry.

The room had also a fireplace with a fire laid, a full coal-scuttle, an excellent arm-chair, a few books on a shelf—and that was all.

The Professor having taken stock of these things, did the foolish thing that we should all do under the circumstances. He went to the big oak door, banged it, rattled it, kicked it, and abused it. It stood firm.

The next thing he did was also a thing which any of us would have done, though it had more sense in it—he shouted at the top of his voice. He kept up that shouting in a number of incongruous forms in which the word " Help " occurred with a frequency that would have been irritating to a hearer had there been one, but audience he had none.

He knocked furiously at either wall of the long room. He turned at last exhausted, and perceived with delight a low door, which he had failed at first

3 *

to notice; it was in the gloom of the far corner. He made for this door. To his delight it opened easily, and revealed beyond it nothing but darkness. There were matches upon the mantelpiece ; he struck one and peered within. He saw a neat little bed, not made by expert women, rather (he thought) by these jailers of his, and through a farther door he saw what might be a bathroom, fairly comfortably appointed.

Such was Professor Higginson's prison. It might have been worse, and to the pure in heart prison can be no confinement for the soul. But either Professor Higginson's heart was not pure or something else was wrong with him, for when he had taken stock of his little luxuries he treated them to a long malediction, the scope and elaboration of which would have surprised him in other days.

*   *   *   *   *

Necessity, which is stronger than the Gods, knows no law, and is also the mother of invention. She is fruitful in stirring the pontifical instinct, the soul of the builder, of the contriver, in man.

Necessity awoke that primal power in the starved Higginsonian soul. When the Professor of Subliminal Consciousness had prowled round and round the room like a caged carnivorous thing some twenty times, seeking an outlet, harbouring disordered schemes, a clear idea suddenly lit up his cloudy mind.

It was glass again! The skylight was made of glass, and glass is a fragile thing!

He stood with his hands in his trouser pockets looking up to that large, slanting window in the roof and taking stock. It was made to open, but the iron rod which raised and lowered it had been disconnected and taken away. He thought he could perceive in certain small dots far above him the heads of screws recently driven in to secure the outer edge of the skylight and make it fast. He estimated the height. Now your Professor of Subliminal Consciousness in general is no dab at this; but that great Governess of the Gods, Necessity, to whom I have already paid eight well-merited compliments, threw him back in this matter also upon the primitive foundations of society, and the Philosopher was astonished to find himself applying the most ancient of measures. He reckoned by his own height taken against the wall. He was a man of six feet. The lowest part of the window was about twice his own height from the floor—a matter of twelve feet; its summit another six or eight.

Then Professor Higginson, having for the first time in his life *measured*, began the ancient and painful but absorbing task of *building* next.

It is the noblest of man's handicrafts! He had heard somewhere that the stretch of a man's arms is about his own height, and in this spread-eagle fashion he measured the bed, the desk, the chairs, the bookshelves.

He carefully put the food down upon the floor

tipped the desk up lengthways on one end. He did this at a terrible strain—and was annoyed to see ink flowing out suddenly and barely missing his trouser leg.

With a strength he had not believed to be in him, he wheeled the iron bed out of the inner room, and managed to get it hoisted by degrees on top of the desk thus inverted. He next hoisted up the arm-chair, getting his head under the seat of it, suffering some pain in his crown before he got it on to the bed. He passed up the three wooden chairs to keep it company, and then with trembling heart but firm will he began to climb.

It is a pity that too profound a study of Subliminal Consciousness destroys Faith, for if the Professor had but believed in God this would have been an admirable opportunity for prayer. Twice in the long ascent he thought the bed was down on the top of him ; twice he felt a trembling that shook his unhappy soul—the floor seemed so far below ! At last he stood triumphant like the first men who conquered the Matterhorn ; he was ready to erect upon so firm a base the last structure he had planned.

Quaint memories of his childhood returned to him as he fixed the wooden chairs one upon the other, and jammed the lowest of them in between the arms of the padded easy-chair, which was to support the whole.

If the first part of the ascent had proved perilous, this last section—the gingerly mounting of a ladder of chair rungs and legs uneasily poised upon a cushioned seat—was as hazardous as ever human experiment had been. The frail structure creaked and trembled beneath him, as, with infinite caution and testing, he swung one long leg after the other up the frail scaffolding. An unworthy eagerness made his heart beat when he was within the last rung of the top chair seat. The glass of the skylight was all but within his reach . . . he could almost touch it with his outstretched hand as he tried the last step.

But already ominously the wooden child of his fancy, the engine he had made, was beginning to betray him. He felt an uneasy swinging in the tower of chairs. He tried to compensate it by too sudden a movement of his body, and then—CRASH ! —and in the tenth of a second all was ruin.

He felt his head striking a rung of wood, a cushion, an iron bar, his hands clutching at a chaotic and cascading ruin of furniture, and he completed his adventure sitting hard upon the floor with the legs of the wooden chairs about him, the stuffed arm-chair upside down within a foot of his head, the iron bedstead hanging at a dangerous slant above the end of the desk, and the wood of this last gaping in a great gash. He had certainly failed.

* * * * *

There is no soul so strong but defeat will check it for a moment. All the long hours remaining of that day, even when he had eaten food and drunk wine, he despaired of any issue.

As darkness closed in on him he raised the energy to get the bed down on to the floor again. He made it up as best he could (the sheets were clean, the pillows comfortable), and he slept.

Upon the Wednesday morning he woke—but now I must play a trick upon the reader, lest worse should befall him. I must beg him to allow the lapse of that Wednesday, and to consider the Professor rising with the first faint dawn of Thursday. Why they should keep him thus confined, how long they intended to do so, whether those fiendish youngsters were determined upon his slow starvation and death, what was happening to that miserable cheque and therefore to his future peace of mind through the whole term of his life, where he was, by what means, if any, he might be restored to the companionship of his kind—all these things did the Professor ruminate one hundred times, and upon none could he come to any conclusion. Such an occupation were monotonous for the reader to follow, and even if he desires to follow it I cannot be at the pains of writing it out ; so here we are on Thursday morning, the 5th of May, forty-eight hours after he, the Philosopher, had Done the Deed and handed that sad forgery to his captors.

If the truth must be told, repose and isolation had done Professor Higginson good.

In the first place, he had read right through the few books he had found set out for him, and thus became thoroughly acquainted for the first time in his life with the poet Milton, the New Testament, and Goschen on Foreign Exchanges, for such was the library which had been provided for him.

As he rose and stretched himself in that disappointing dawn, he found the energy to go through his empty ceremony of howling for aid, but it soon palled and his throat began to hurt him.

He looked up again at that skylight showing clear above the half darkness of the room, and was struck quite suddenly with a really brilliant scheme. He remembered bitterly the painful misfortune of his first attempt, rubbed a sore place, and wished to Heaven that his present revelation had come first.

He proceeded to execute at once the promptings of his new scheme. He took the sheets of his bed and tied them one to another, the pillow cases he linked up upon the tail of these, and, to make certain of the whole matter, he ended by tying on the counterpane as well. He tied them all securely together, for he intended the rope so made to bear his whole weight. Taking one of the broken chairs, he secured it stoutly to one end of the line ; he chose his position carefully beneath the skylight, he swung the chair, and at the end of the third swing hurled it up into the air at the glass above him. It was his plan to break that glass. The chair would catch upon the ridge of the roof outside, and he would manage in his desperation to swarm up the tied sheets and win his way through the broken pane to the roof. The chair was heavy, and he failed some twenty times. Twice the chair had struck him heavily on the head as it fell back, but he persevered.

Perseverance is the one virtue which the Gods reward, and at long last the Professor saw and heard his missile crashing clean through the skylight. He was as good as free, save that—such is the academic temper !—he had forgotten to catch hold of the other end of the line

He heard the chair rattle loudly down the roof outside, he saw its long tail of knotted sheets swiftly drawn up through the broken skylight, he leapt up to clutch it just too late, and marked in despair the last of his bedclothes flashing up past and above him like a white snake, to disappear through the broken window from his gaze. Two seconds afterwards he heard the chair fall into the garden some fifty feet below, and he noted with some disgust that a quantity of broken glass had come down upon his food.

It was, as I have said, in the first grey light of the third day—the Thursday—that he had thus gratuitously shed his bedding. For some moments after that failure he sat down and despaired. He also felt his head where the chair had struck it.

As he turned round helplessly to discover whether some object might not suggest a further plan, he was astonished to see the great oaken door standing ajar. He pulled it open to its widest extent ; the green baize door beyond swung to his touch, and he was a free man.

Someone had slipped those bolts in the night, and if that someone were Jimmy, Jimmy had kept his word.

It was with no gratitude that Professor Higginson

cautiously and fearfully descended the stairs. He
knew so little of men, that he dreaded further capture
and some vigorous young scoundrel leaping upon
him from an unexpected door. He passed three
flights, each untenanted, furnitureless, and quite
silent, until he reached the hall.

The front door stood wide open. The delicious
breath of the early summer morning came in, mixed
with the twittering of birds. Still wondering and
half doubting his good fortune, Professor Higginson
was about to step out, when he remembered—what ?
—the *Green Overcoat*. He must face the ordeal of
those stairs again. It was the bravest thing he had
ever done in his life. It was the only brave thing he
had ever done in his life. But fear of worse things
compelled him. If that Green Overcoat were found
and he were traced—he dared not think of the
consequences.

His recent experience was far too vivid for him to
dream of putting it on. He carried the great weight
of it over his arm, and in the first steps he took in the
open air towards the lodge, under that pure sky, in
which the sun had not yet risen, it was his honest
and his firm intention to take it straight to
Crampton Park, to discover " Lauderdale," to restore
it to its owner and to explain all.

The lodge he found to be empty and even ruinous.
A mouldy gate stood with one of its bars broken,
hanging by a single hinge, ajar. He passed out upon
a lonely country lane. He was glad it was lonely.
An elderly don in an exceedingly dirty shirt, clad in

evening clothes which had been through something
worse than a prize fight, his collar crumpled and vile,
no tie, and boots half buttonless, would be foolish to
desire any general companionship of human strangers
upon a May-day morning.   It was up to him to find
his whereabouts, and to make the best of his way to
his lodgings and to proper clothing.   Then, he hoped,
by six at the latest, he could do what the voice of
duty bade him do.   He felt in his pocket, and was
glad to find his latch-key and his money safe, for
with these two a man commands the world ; but as
he felt in his pockets he missed something familiar.
What it was he could not recollect—only, he knew
vaguely, something he expected was not there, a
memorandum or what not.   He set it down for
nervousness, and went his way.

The rolling landscape of the Midlands was to his
left and right.   The lane ran along a ridge that
commanded some little view upon either side.   It
led him northwards, and he could see in the clear
air, for the moment smokeless, the tall chimneys of
Ormeston.   They were perhaps five miles away, and
the Professor prepared to cover that distance.   His
heart was shot with a varied emotion, of exultation
at his morning freedom, of terror that his evil
deeds might have gone before him.   But he was
determined upon his duty under that cold dawn.
He went swinging forward.

The east put on its passing cloudless colours, and
beyond the rim of fields, far outward beyond the
world, Phœbus Apollo rose unheralded and shone

with his first level beams upon the misguided man.

Now almost as Apollo rose, whether proceeding from Apollo's influence or from that of some Darker Power, hesitation and scheming entered once more into the heart of Professor Higginson.

First, he found that he was getting a little tired of the way. Five miles was a long distance. Then he remembered his determination to give up the Coat. It was heavy. Why carry it five miles and make a fool of himself at the end of them?

By the second mile he had come to the conclusion that it was ridiculous to knock up what was probably a wealthy merchant's household ("Lauderdale" sounded like that, so did Crampton Park) at such unearthly hours. The man was certainly wealthy —he had seen his name in the papers when he had got his chair a few months before.

In the third mile Mr. Higginson determined not to fulfil his difficult mission until he had groomed himself and could call upon this local bigwig at a reasonable hour. Such men (he remembered) were influential in provincial towns.

In the midst of the fourth mile he saw before him the first of the tall standards which marked the end of an electric tramway, and at that point stood a shelter, very neat, provided by some local philanthropic scoundrel. It sent up a grateful little curl of smoke which promised coffee.

The Professor came to the door of the shelter, timidly turned its handle, and peered in.

Three men were within. Two seemed to be night-watchmen, one of whom was concocting the brew, the other cutting large slices of bread and butter. The third man—short, stubby, and of an expression wholly dull and vicious—was not in their uniform. He had the appearance of a man whose profession was very vague, and seemed to be lounging there for no better purpose than cadging a cup from pals. He was remarkable for nothing but a Broken Nose.

The Professor smelt the delicious steam. He came in through the doorway, and all three men looked up.

It is a beautiful trait in our national character that the poor will ever welcome the wealthier classes, particularly when these betray upon their features that sort of imbecile ignorance of reality and childish trust in rogues which is common to all the liberal professions save that of the law, which is rare in merchants, which is universal in dons.

If the mass of our people love a guileless simplicity in their superiors, when it is accompanied by debauch they positively adore it ; and the excellent reception the Professor met with upon his entry was due more than anything else to the conviction of his three inferiors that an elderly man in tattered evening clothes and abominable linen must have spent the night before in getting outrageously drunk.

His offer of no less than a shilling for a piece of bread and a cup of coffee was gratefully accepted. The word " Sir " was used at least eighteen times in the first three minutes of conversation.

The Professor felt that he was with friends, and his self-discipline weakened and weakened by degree after degree. It sank with the coffee and the bread, it sank lower with the respectful tones in which he was addressed ; then without warning it vanished, and that soul which had already fallen to forgery and intemperate language went down a further step to Sheol.

The Devil, who had been away during the last two days attending to other business, must have caught the Professor as he passed that lodge-gate and have hastened to his side. At any rate, Mr. Higginson deliberately sized up the three men before him, determined with justice that the lounger, the Man with the Broken Nose, was the most corruptible and at the same time the least dangerous if anything should come to the (dreadful word !) police.

He led up to his subject carefully. He said that Crampton Park was in the neighbourhood, was it not ? He had heard that it lay somewhere to the left in a western suburb of the town. He professed to have found the Green Overcoat in the hall of the house where—where he had passed the night, and as he used these words the three toilers discreetly smiled. He professed to have promised to return it. He professed to remember—with grateful un-expectedness—the name of the house to which he had promised to send it. It was " Lauderdale." He professed an ignorance of the name of its owner. The Professor professed far more that morning of sin than his academic professorship entitled him to do.

He found the lounger (with the Broken Nose) somewhat indifferent to his motives, but very much alive to the economics of the situation ; and when the bargain was struck it was for half a crown that the bad proletarian man (with the Broken Nose) took the Green Overcoat over his disreputable arm, promising to deliver it at " Lauderdale " in the course of the morning.

An immense weight was lifted from the unworthy mind of Professor Higginson. Must I tell the whole of the shameful tale ? The Professor, as he rose to leave the Shelter, positively added to his fellow-citizen of the Broken Nose—

" Oh ! And by the way ! Of course, he will ask who the Coat is from. . . . Say it is from Mr. Hitchenbrook." He pretended to feel in his pocket. " No, I haven't got a card ; anyhow, say Mr. Hitchenbrook — Mr. Hitchenbrook, of Cashington," he added genially, to round off the wicked lie.

Thus relieved of duty and thus divorced from Heaven, Professor Higginson nodded authoritatively to the Broken Nose, cheerfully to the other two men (who touched their hair with their forefingers in reply), and strode out again to follow the tram lines into the town.

*   *   *   *   *

Now here, most upright of readers, you will say that the Philosopher has fallen to his lowest depth,

and that no further crime he may commit can entertain you.

You are in error.   The depths of evil are infinite,
and the Professor, as he walked down the long road
which brought him to Ormeston, was but entering
that long road of the spirit which leads to full
damnation.

CHAPTER VI

*In which Professor Higginson Begins to Taste
the Sweets of Fame*

WHEN Professor Higginson reached the door of his
lodgings the Ormeston day had begun.

The house was one of a row of eighteenth-century
buildings, dignified and a trifle decayed, representing
in the geology of the town the strata of its first
mercantile fortunes. It was here that the first
division between the rich and poor of industrial
Ormeston had begun to show itself four generations
ago, and these roomy, half-deserted houses were the
first fruits of that economic change.

But Professor Higginson was not thinking of all
that as he came up to the well-remembered door
(which in the despair of the past nights he had
sometimes thought he would never see again). He
was thinking of how he looked with his horribly
crushed and dirty shirt front, his ruined collar, and·
his bedraggled evening clothes upon that bright
morning. In this reflection he was aided by the
fixed stares of the young serving-maids who were
cleaning the doorsteps and the unrestrained remarks
of youths who passed him in their delivery of milk.
The first with their eyes, the second more plainly

with their lips, expressed the opinion that he was no longer of an age for wanton pleasures, and he was annoyed and flustered to hear himself compared to animals of a salacious kind, notably the goat.

It was not to be wondered at that, being what he was, a man who had never had to think or act in his life, Professor Higginson's one desire was to put his familiar door between himself and such tormentors.

He rang the bell furiously and knocked more furiously still. An errand-boy, a plumber's apprentice upon his way to work, and a road scavenger joined a milkman, and watched him at this exercise in a little group. It was a group which threatened to become larger, for Ormeston is an early town. Professor Higginson, forgetting that Mrs. Randle, his landlady, might not be up at such an hour, gave another furious assault upon the knocker, suddenly remembered his latch key, brought it out, and was nervously feeling for the keyhole amid jeers upon his aim, when the door was suddenly opened and the considerable figure of Mrs. Randle appeared in the passage.

For one moment she looked as people are said to look at ghosts that return from Hell, then with a shriek that startled the echoes of the whole street, she fell heavily against the Professor's unexpecting form, nearly bringing it down the steps.

Mr. Higginson was guilty of a nervous movement of repulsion. A little more and he would have succeeded in shaking off the excellent but very weighty woman who had thus greeted his return, but even as he did so he heard the odious comments of the Ormeston chivalry, notably the milkman, who told him not to treat his wife like a savage. The plumber also called it cruel. It was therefore with some excuse that the great Psychologist thrust the lady of the house within and slammed the door behind him with his heel.

Mrs. Randle was partially recovered, but still woefully shaken. He got past her brutally enough, pushed into the ground floor room in the front of the house, and sat down. He felt the exhaustion of his walk and the irritation of the scene which had just passed to be too much for him. Mrs. Randle, with a large affection, stood at the table before him, leaning heavily upon it with her fists, and saying, "Oh, sir!" consecutively several times, until her emotion was sufficiently calm to permit of rational speech. Then she asked him where he had been.

"It's the talk of the whole town, sir! Oh! and me too! Never, I never thought to see you again!" at which point in her interrogation Mrs. Randle broke suddenly into a flood of tears, punctuated by sobs as explosive as they were sincere.

She sat down the better to enjoy this relief, and even as she had risen to its climax, and the Professor was being moved to louder and louder objurgation, the bell rang and the hammer knocked in a way that was not to be denied. The unfortunate man caught what glimpse he could from the window, and was horrified to see two officers of the law supported by a crowd grown to respectable dimensions, the foremost members of which were giving accurate information upon all that had happened.

The Philosopher summoned the manhood to open the door and to face his accusers. They were not so startled as Mrs. Randle, who now came up with red and tearful face and somewhat out of breath (but her weeping largely overlain with indignation) to protest against the violation of her house.

The first of the policemen had hardly begun his formal questioning of Professor Higginson, when the second, looking a little closer, recognised his prey. That subtle air which no civilian can hope to possess, and by which, like the savages of Central Africa, the British police convey thought without words or message, acted at once upon the second man, and he adopted a manner of the utmost respect. To prove his zeal he dispersed the crowd of loungers, saluted, and told the Professor that it was his duty to ask him formally certain questions ; whereat his colleague—he that had first recognised the great man —added with equal humility that as Mr. Higginson had been lost, and the University moving the police in the matter, it was only their duty to ask what they should do, and what light Mr. Higginson could throw on the affair. There was a report of fighting. To this Mrs. Randle interposed, without a trace of logic, " Fighting yourself ! "

The Professor was very glad to answer any questions that might be put to him, and very much relieved when he found that these were no more than what the police required to trace the misadventure of so prominent a citizen : at whose hand he had suffered, or what adventure had befallen him ; was it murder —but they saw it was not that ; whether the reward which had been offered should be withdrawn, and what clues the Professor could furnish.

Mr. Higginson looked blankly at these men, then his eyes lit with anger. He was upon the very point of pouring out the whole story of his woes, when with that cold wind upon the heart which the condemned feel 'when they awake to reality upon the morning of execution, he remembered the cheque and was suddenly silent.

" You 'd better leave me ! " he muttered. " You 'd better leave me, officer ! "

" We *were* instructed, sir," began the senior man more respectfully than ever—then Professor Higginson bolted to refuge.

" Well, I will see you in a minute ; I must put myself right. I am all —— "

" We quite understand, sir," said the policemen, taking their stations in the ground floor room, and drawing chairs as with the intention of sitting down and awaiting his pleasure.

" I will see you when I can. Mrs. Randle, please bring me some hot water."

And with these words the poor man dashed upstairs to his bedroom upon the first floor.

There are ways of defeating a woman's will when she has passed the age of forty, and these are described in books which deal either with an imaginary world of fiction or with a remote and unattainable past. No living man has dealt with the art, nor can wizards show you an example of it.

Therefore, when Mrs. Randle returned with the hot water, it was Mrs. Randle that won.

The Professor poked his head through the door and reached out for the can. Mrs. Randle broke his centre, marched for the washhand stand, poured out the grateful liquid, tempered it with cold, motherly tested its temperature with her large red hand, and the while opened fire with a rattle of questions, particularly begging of him not to tell her anything until he was quite rested. Of course, there were the police (she said), and she would have to tell her own tale, too, and oh, dear, if he only knew what it had been those days! With the Mayor himself, and what not! At each stage in her operations she was careful to threaten a fit of crying.

Professor Higginson's tactics were infantile. They were those of his sex. He took off his coat and waistcoat preparatory to washing. Upon minor occasions in the past, mere affairs of outposts, Mrs. Randle had taken cover before this manœuvre ; to-day the occasion was decisive, and she stood firm.

" ——and the Principal of the University too, sir ! And his dear young lady ! And, oh ! when they put that news in the paper, which wasn't true, thanks be to God ——"

Here, as Mrs. Randle approached tears again, the desperate philosopher threw his braces from his shoulders, plunged his face and hands into the water, and fondly hoped that when he lifted it again the enemy would have fled. But Mrs. Randle was a widow, and the first sound he heard as the water ran out of his ears was the continuing string of lamentations and questionings.

"Where's the towel?" he asked abruptly.

"Where it's been since last Monday, sir," said Mrs. Randle. "Since that last Blessed Monday when we thought to lose you for ever! I never thought to change it! I never thought to see you back all of a heap like this!"

"Last Monday?" hesitated Mr. Higginson genuinely enough. His calendar had got a little muddled. "What's to-day?" he said it easily. Then he saw a look on her face.

There is a rank in society in which to forget the day of the week has a very definite connotation—it means . . . it means something wrong with the Brain. Like a flash an avenue of salvation was suggested to the hunted man by Mrs. Randle's look. He could *lose* those few days! They could disappear from his life—utterly—and with them that accursed business of the Green Overcoat and the fatal cheque-book it had hidden in its man-destroying folds!

In the very few seconds which creative work will take under the influence of hope and terror, the scheme began to elaborate itself in the narrow mind of the poor, persecuted don. He flopped down upon a chair, paused suddenly in the vigorous rubbing of his face with the towel, passed his hand over the baldness of his forehead, and muttered vacantly—

" Where am I ? "

" You 're here, sir ! Oh, you 're here ! " said good, kind Mrs. Randle in an agonised tone, positively going down upon her knees (no easy thing when religion has departed with youth) and laying one hand upon his knee.

The Professor laid his left hand upon hers, passed his right hand again over his face, and gasped in a thin voice—

" Where 's here ? "

" In Quebec Street in your own room, sir ! Oh, sir, don't you know me ? I 'm Martha Randle ? "

The Professor looked down at her with weary but forgiving eyes.

" I do now," he said ; " it comes back to me."

" Oh, Lord ! " said Martha Randle, " I 'll send the girl for the chemist ! " and she was gone.

Women may be stronger than we men, my brothers, but we are more cunning ; and when she had gone the Professor, dropping the mask and dressing with extreme alacrity, made himself possible in morning clothes. His plan had developed still further in the few minutes it took him to go downstairs, and as he entered the room where the policemen awaited him, he was his own master and theirs.

They rose at his entrance. He courteously bade them be seated again, and not allowing them to get any advantage of the first word, told them the plain truth in a few simple and cultivated sentences, such as could not but carry conviction to any insufficiently salaried official.

"I think it well, officer," he said, addressing the senior of the two men, "to tell you the truth here privately. I will, of course, put the whole thing later before the proper authorities."

The policemen looked grave and acquiescent.

"The fact is," replied Professor Higginson rapidly, "I had been working very hard at my Address—which you may have heard of."

The two men looked at once as though they had.

"It was for the Bergson Society," he explained courteously, and the older policeman nodded as though he were a member himself.

"Well," went on Professor Higginson in the tone of a man who must out with it at last, "the fact is, there followed—there followed, I am sorry to say, there followed something like a stroke—at any rate, bad nervous trouble. . . . *I have suffered— apparently for some days—from a complete loss of memory.*"

And having put the matter plainly and simply in such a fashion, Professor Higginson was silent.

"We quite understand, sir," said the senior of the two policemen gravely, sympathetically and respectfully. "There shan't be a word from us, sir, except of course ——"

"*No,*" said Professor Higginson firmly, "I am determined to do my duty in this matter; those whom it is proper to tell ——"

At this moment Mrs. Randle, accompanied by a half-dressed servant, herself in an untied bonnet and somewhat out of breath, was heard at the open door with the reluctant and sleepy chemist, who was her medical adviser.

"And he was that bad he thought I was his poor old mother, who's been dead these twenty years!" went on Mrs. Randle's voice outside.

But a moment afterwards, as she came into the inner room, she saw the Professor seated and clothed and in his right mind. He rejected her exuberance.

"Now, Mrs. Randle," he said rather sharply, and forgetting for a moment the natural nervous weakness to be expected of one who had suffered Such Things, "I have told the officers here and I desire you to know it as well."

He glanced at the chemist, rapidly decided that the more people knew his tale the better, and said with intentional flattery—

"I thank you, sir, for coming; you are a medical man."

Then he continued, turning to the policemen again—

"You understand? There is unfortunately very little to say. My last recollection is of leaving Sir John Perkin's house—he was giving a party on— on . . . wait a moment . . . it was *Monday*. I remember having a sort of shock just after getting out of his gate, and then I do not remember anything more until I was approaching this house. It will be Tuesday to-day?"

"No, sir," said the policeman, with grave reverence for one so learned, so distinguished, and at the same time so unique in misfortune. It reminded

4

him of the wonderful things in the Sunday papers, and he believed. " No, sir ; to-day is Thursday."

" *Thursday ?* " said the Professor, affecting bewilderment with considerable skill. " Thursday ? " he repeated, turning to the chemist, who said solemnly—

" Thursday, sir ! "

" Oh, poor dear ! " immediately howled Mrs. Randle.

" Be quiet," shouted Professor Higginson very rudely. " If it is Thursday," he continued to the others, dropping his voice again, " this is a more serious thing than I had imagined. Why, three whole days . . . and yet, wait ——" (and here he extended one hand and covered his eyes with the other) " I seem to have an impression of . . . cold meat . . . a room . . . voices . . . no, it is gone."

The younger policeman pulled out a note-book and an extremely insufficient pencil, which was at once short, thick and bald-headed.

" Lost any valuables, sir ? " he began.

The Professor slapped his pockets, and then suddenly remembered that he had changed his clothes.

" No," he mused. " No, not to my knowledge. I had my watch " (he began to tick off on his fingers) " and a few shillings change . . ." But for the life of him he couldn't decide whether to lose valuables or not. On the whole he decided not to.

" No " (after careful thought), " no, I lost nothing.

My boots were very damp as I took them off, if that
is any clue."

The younger policeman was rapidly putting it all
down in the official shorthand. Habit compelled
him to make the outline, " The Prisoner persistently
denied ——" He scratched it out and put, " The
Professor told us that he had not ——" Then came
the second question—

" In what part of the town, sir, might it be that
you knew yourself again, sir, so to speak ? "

" I have told you, close by here," said Professor
Higginson.

" Yes, but coming which way like ? "

Here was a magnificent opening ! He had never
thought of that. He considered what was the most
central quarter of the town, what least suggested a
suburb. He remembered a dirty old mid-Victorian
church, now the cathedral, in the heart of the city,
and he said—

" St. Anne's, it was close to St. Anne's."

Then he remembered—most luckily—that there
were witnesses to his having come up the street from
exactly the opposite quarter, and he added—

" At least that 's where I began to remember a
little ; but I wandered about, I didn't remember
the street for a good hour, and even when I came
here I was still troubled . . . Mrs. Randle will
tell you ——"

" Oh," began Mrs. Randle, " Lord knows he gave
a cry that loud on seeing me——" but the policeman
did not want to hear this.

He put this third question—

"About what time might this be?"

"About," said the Professor, speaking slowly but thinking at his fastest, "about . . . about three hours ago. It was still dark. It was getting light. I remember going through the streets, getting a little clearer from time to time as to what I was doing and where I was."

The manœuvre was not without wisdom. Had he made the time shorter there would have been inquiries, and they might have lit upon the three men in the shelter, and that detestable Green Overcoat might have come in once more to ruin his life. As it was, whoever the middle-aged person in battered evening clothes may have been who had entered the shelter on that morning, it could not be *he*. The policeman strapped the elastic over his note-book again.

"That'll do, sir," he said kindly.

Mrs. Randle was swift to find a couple of glasses of beer, which beverage the uncertain hours of their profession permit the constabulary to consume at any period whatsoever of the day or night, and what I may call "The Great Higginson Lost Memory Case" started on its travels round the world.

During the remainder of that day—the Thursday —Professor Higginson was prodigal enough of his experience. It was a great thing for a Professor of Subliminal Psychology to have come in direct touch in this way with one of the most interesting of psychical phenomena. Everyone he met in the

next hours had a question to ask, and every question
did Professor Higginson meet with a strange facility ;
but, alas ! with renewed and more complex untruth.
Had he *any* recollections ?   Yes . . . Yes.
Were there faces ?   Yes, there were faces.   Drawn
faces.   He could say more (he hinted), for the thing
was still sacred to him.

One cross-questioned a little too closely about the
sense of *Time*.   Had he an idea of its flight during
that singular vision ?   Yes.   Yes. . . . In a way.
He remembered a conversation—a long one—and a
flight : a flight through space.

What ! a flight through space ?

He told the story with much fuller details that very
morning about noon to his most intimate personal
friend, the editor of the second paper in Ormeston.

He told it again at the club at lunch to a small
audience with the zest of a man who is describing a
duel of his.   He told it to a larger audience over
coffee after lunch.   He went back to arrange matters
at the University, and to say that he could take up
his work the next morning.

It was to the Dean (who was also a Professor
of Chemistry), to the Vice-Principal, and to the
Chaplain that he had to unbosom himself on this
official occasion.   All were curious, and by the time
they had cheered him, the desperate man's relation
had grown to be one of the most exact and beautiful
little pieces of modern psychical experience conceiv-
able.   All the functionings of the sub-conscious man
in the absence of a co - ordinating consciousness

were falling into place, and the World that is beyond this World had been visited by the least likely of the sons of men.

As one detail suggested another, the necessity for a coherent account bred what mere experience could never have done.

Now and then in these conversations Professor Higginson thought he heard a note of doubt in some inquirer's voice. It spurred him to new confirmations, new lies.

For his mathematical colleague he swore to the fourth dimension ; for his historical one, to a conspectus of time. " Little windows into the past," he called it, the horrid man !

Then—then in a moment of whirl he did the fatal thing. It was a Research man called Garden who goaded him.

Garden had said—

" What *were* the faces ? What *were* the voices ? How did they differ from dreams ? "

Professor Higginson felt the spur point.

" Garden," he said, facing that materialist with a marvellously solemn look, " Garden . . . How do you know reality ? I *saw* . . . I *heard*." He shuddered successfully. " Garden," he went on abruptly, " have you ever loved one—who died ? "

" Bless you, yes ! " answered Garden cheerfully.

" Garden ! " continued the Philosopher in a deep but shaken voice, " I too have lost where I loved— and " (he almost whispered the rest) " and *we held communion during that brief time*."

"What!" said Garden. He stared at the tall, lanky Professor of Psychology. He didn't believe, not a word. But it was the first time he had come across that sort of lunacy, and it shocked him. "*What!* The Dead?"

Mr. Higginson nodded twice with fixed lips and far-away eyes.

"There is proof," he said, and was gone.

*   *   *   *   *

Garden stared after him, then he shrugged his shoulders, muttered, "Mad as a hatter!" and turned to go his way. It was about five o'clock.

*   *   *   *   *

Among other things which the Devil had done in that period with which this story deals was the planting in Ormeston of a certain servant of his, by name George Babcock.

George Babcock had come to Ormeston after a curious and ill-explained, a short and a decisive episode in life. He had begun as a young theorist, who had startled Europe from the foreign University where he was studying by a thesis now forgotten abroad, but one the memory of which still lingered in England, for a paper had boomed it.

It had been a scornful and triumphant refutation of the Hypnotists of Nancy.

George Babcock had rolled the Nancy school over and over, and for a good five years the young English writer, with his perfect command of German, had been the prophet of common sense. "Hypnotism," as that school called their charlatanry, was done for, a series of clumsy frauds, a thing of illusions, special apparatus and lies.

Unfortunately for civilisation, the superstitions of the Hypnotists, as we know, prevailed, and European science has grown ashamed since that day of its earlier and manlier standpoint. It. has learnt to talk of auto-suggestion. It has fallen so low as to be interested in Lourdes.

Long before 1890 George Babcock's book was ruined abroad. But George Babcock was a man with a knowledge of the road, and while his reputation, dead upon the Continent, was at its height in England, he suddenly appeared, no longer as a theorist, but as a practising doctor in London. He had borrowed the money for the splash on the strength of that English reputation, which he retained, and for ten years he was a Big Man. It was said that he had saved a great deal of money. He certainly made it. Then there came—no one knows what. The professionals who were most deeply in the know hinted at a quarrel with Great Ladies upon the secrets of his trade—and theirs.

At any rate, for another three years after the little episode, George Babcock's name took a new and inferior position in the Daily Press. It appeared in the lists of City dinners, at meetings, at the head of middle-class "leagues" and "movements" that failed. When it was included in the list of a country-house party that party would not be of quite the first flight, and, what was terribly significant to those few who can look with judgment and pity on the modern world, articles signed by the poor fellow began to appear in too great a quantity in the magazines. He even published three books. It was very sad.

Then came the incorporation of the University of Ormeston, or, as people preferred to call it from those early days, the Guelph University, after the name of a patron, and the Prime Minister's private secretary had been sent to suggest, as the head of the Medical School, the name of George Babcock.

He was neither a knight nor a baronet, but Ormeston did not notice that. The old glamour of his name lingered in that prosperous town. A married cousin of the Mayor of that year, whose wife dined out in London, reported his political power. The merchants and the rest in the newly-formed Senate of the University timidly approached the Great Man, and the Great Man jumped at it.

He had now for five years been conducting his classes at the absurdly low salary of £900 a year.

George Babcock remained after all his escapades and alarms—such as they may have been—a man of energy and of singular organising power, an Atheist of course, and one possessed both of clear mental vision and a sort of bodily determination that would not fail him until his body failed. His face and his shoulders were square, his jaw too was strong, the looseness of his thick mouth was what one would expect from what was known about him by those who knew. His eyes were fairly steady, occasionally

4 *

sly ; his brows and forehead handsomely clean ; his hair thick and strongly grey.

This was the figure Garden saw coming up the street towards him as Professor Higginson shambled off, already a distant figure, nearing the gates of the College (for it was in the street without that the Philosopher had met the Research man and made that fatal move).

To say that Garden was glad to meet Babcock would be to put it too strongly ; no one was ever glad to meet Babcock. But to say that he was indifferent to the chance of blabbing would not be true ; no one is indifferent to the chance of blabbing.

" I say, Babcock," he said, checking the advancing figure with his raised hand, " old Higginson 's gone mad."

Babcock smiled uglily.

" Yes, he has," said Garden, " saying all sorts of things about that little trouble he had. Saw ghosts ! "

" They all do," said Babcock grimly.

" Oh, yes, I know," answered Garden, eager for the importance of his tale, " but he 's got it all pat ! Says he can prove it ! "

Garden nodded mysteriously.

" He gave me some details, you know," went on Garden most irresponsibly ; then he pulled himself up. He wanted to have something important to say, but he was a nervous man in handling those tarradiddles which are the bulk of interesting conversation.

Babcock looked sceptical.

" What sort of details ? " he sneered.

" Oh, I 'm not allowed to tell you," said Garden uneasily, " but it was very striking, really it was."

Then suddenly he broke away. He felt he might be led on, and he didn't want to make a fool of himself. He rather wished he hadn't spoken. Babcock let him go, and as Garden disappeared in his turn the Doctor paced more slowly. He was not disturbed, but he was interested.

Everyone in the University had heard about Higginson's Spiritual Experience, everyone was already talking of it ; that wasn't the odd part. The odd part (he mused) was a man like Garden taking it seriously. . . .

The more Mr. Babcock thought of it the more favourably a certain possibility presented itself.

He made his way towards the telephone-room at the Porter's Lodge, asked them to call up a number in London, and waited patiently until he obtained it.

He took the full six minutes, and it will interest those who reverence our ancient constitution to know that the person to whom George Babcock was talking was a peer—one of those few peers who live at the end of a wire, and not only a peer but the owner of many things.

The man at the other end of the wire was the owner of railway shares innumerable, for the moment of stores of wheat (for he was gambling in that), but in particular of many newspapers, chief of which a sheet which had thrust back into their corners all

older, milder things, and had come to possess the
mind of England. This premier newspaper was
called *The Howl;* nor did the writer of that letter
own *The Howl* only, but altogether some eighty
other rags ; nor in this country only was he feared,
though he was more feared in this country than in
any other. .

It was his boast that he could make and unmake
men, and every politician in turn had blacked his
boots, and he had made judges, and had at times
decided upon peace and war. A powerful man ;
known to his gutter (before he bought his peerage)
as Mr. Cake ; a flabby man—and vulgar ? Oh !
my word !

This man at the other end of the wire knew much,
too much, about George Babcock, and George
Babcock knew that he knew it. From time to time
George Babcock, sickening at the recollection of
such knowledge privy only to him and to his lordship,
was moved to services which, had he been a free man,
he would not have undertaken. He was about to
perform such a service now.

He told the story briefly to that telephone receiver.
He insisted on the value of it. The man at the other
end of the wire was very modern. He had a list of
the expresses before him. He told George Babcock
to expect a letter that would come up by the six
o'clock and reach Ormeston at 8.5. George Babcock
would get his instructions by that train. At 8.5,
therefore, George Babcock, bound to service and
not over-willing, was on the platform, took the

packet from the guard, feed him, opened it, and read.

The letter was not type-written. It was a familiar letter, and it was signed of course by a single un-initialed name, for was not its author a peer?

*   *   *   *   *

Meanwhile, the unfortunate Professor of Psychology was wandering within the College buildings from room to room, from friend to friend, and spreading everywhere as he went a long and tortuous train of falsehood and of doom.

Just before dinner, sitting with the Vice-Principal's wife in her drawing-room, he added one very beautiful little point which had previously escaped him—how during what must have been the middle of his curious trance he had heard the most heavenly singing—he who could not tell one note from another on ordinary days! The Chaplain had already used him before ten o'clock as a proof of the immortality of the soul in his notes for next Sunday's sermon, and a local doctor had been particularly interested to hear, as they met just before dinner, that though he *may* have had food and drink during that long period, the only thing he could remember was cold meat, and that only as something seen, not as something consumed.

"What kind of cold meat?" the doctor had said; but Professor Higginson, whose brain was not of the poet's type, had only answered, "Oh, just cold meat."

Thus by the evening of that Thursday was the dread process of publicity begun.

That night, while all slept, in the two Ormeston newspaper offices, shut up in their little dog kennels, the leader writers were scribbling away at top speed, dealing with Subliminal Consciousness and the Functions Unco-ordinated by Self-cognisant Co-ordination, the one from the Conservative, the other from the Liberal standpoint.

Even the Socialist weekly paper which went to press on Friday was compelled to have a note upon the subject ; but knowing that it must bring in some reference to the nationalisation of the means of production *and* the Parsonic Fraud, it basely said that Professor Higginson was, like every other supporter of the Bourgeois State, a so-called Christian, in which slander, as I need hardly inform the reader, there was not a word of truth.

And so, having dined well with his Vice-Principal and had his fill, Professor Higginson set out by night to seek his lodgings.

CHAPTER VII

In which Professor Higginson goes on tasting them

PROFESSOR HIGGINSON was glad to get back to his lodgings on that Thursday night ; he was beginning to feel the weariness of the Lion.

I will not deny that some vanity had arisen in him, for he felt the approach of a little local fame. Now vanity, especially when it is connected with the approach of a little local fame, is not good for Professors, even in this world ; for their chances in the next it is fatal. It is a foible only too acceptable as an instrument to the Enemy of Souls.

Full of this vague sensation of well-being, it was a shock to Professor Higginson to find George Babcock waiting for him in his rooms.

Hidden in the right - hand pocket of George Babcock's coat was the letter. It was not type-written. It was a familiar letter. It was signed by a single uninitialed name, for its author was a peer.

Higginson came into the room nervously, less and less pleased to see who his visitor was, but that visitor had something very definite to do.

" I say, Higginson," he cried suddenly, rising as suddenly at his colleague's entry into the room, " you know I don't believe a word of it ! "

" A word of what ? " said Higginson tartly.

"Oh, you know," said Babcock, sitting down again as did Higginson also, and fixing the psychologist with his strong eyes. " You 've told everybody, and everybody 's talking. All this ' psychical experience,' Higginson ! All these—damn it. why you 're talking *ghosts* now ! "

He sat back and waited.

" Babcock," said Higginson, in much the same tones as he had used to fire upon the less defended Mr. Garden, " Babcock, you won't believe a plain human tale ? The Evidence of a witness ? *True* evidence, Babcock ? "

"Oh, I believe you had some—some, well, let 's say some mental experience, all right ; but I don't believe in all that monkey business. . . . No !
. . . I 'm interested, Higginson. That 's why I 've come." He leant forward. " I 'm *really* interested."

" You don't believe that I saw . . . what I say I saw ? " said Higginson solemnly.

" Why, my dear Higginson, you know—one *sees* things when one 's asleep. Simple ? "

" You don't believe," reiterated Higginson, " that I heard what I *say* I heard ? "

"Oh, I believe that right enough," answered Babcock impatiently. " What 's ' hearing ' ? My dear fellow, for one case of optical suggestion there are ten cases of aural ! "

" Suggestion be —— ! " cried Professor Higginson too suddenly.

" It 's a funny thing, Higginson," said Babcock,
looking curiously at him and pinning his colleague
down with that look, " it 's a funny thing that you
spook Johnnies don't seem to know what evidence
is. . . . Ever heard a clever counsel briefed in
Poison ? . . . I have."

" I——" began Professor Higginson, but Babcock
interrupted.

" Now, I knew a fellow once in Italy, not like you,
my dear Higginson, not half so honest a man, but
he *had* got hold of what convinces people. . . .
It 's not what 's true, it 's what convinces."

Babcock smiled oddly as he said this.

" He didn't publish it . . . and " (this more
slowly) " I will tell you what it was, for it impressed
me. He came into my room early one morning—I
knew him well enough—and he told me the whole
story of Adowa. The telegraph hadn't brought it,
Higginson " (shaking a finger). " We hadn't heard
of it. No one in Europe, no one in Egypt. The
fight was . . . well, 'lowing for longitude . . .
not twelve hours old. And, mind you, he didn't
give a sort of hint ; he didn't work your telepathy
stunt." Babcock began to emphasise. " He
described the whole thing quite clearly : with little
men and bushes and hot sand standing clear, like
three or four little *coloured* pictures. Eh ? *Coloured.*
Painted. You could *smell* the heat. And he saw a
sort of local storm on the scrub in the valley ; he
did !—least, he *said* he did ! He saw the poor fellows
left behind—the wounded, you know : he saw the

faces of the torturers." Babcock stopped a second and changed his tone. He looked unpleasantly in earnest. "He told me I might make money over it," he went on. "I was in touch with one of the English papers. Like a fool, I didn't believe him. After that the telegrams came in . . ."

⋆ Professor Higginson was watching his colleague; his head stood forward on his long neck. He was fascinated and a little frightened.

"Well," said Babcock, sitting down and speaking with less apparent purpose, "that's all. I think he was a charlatan. I don't know how he got the thing. I 've known news spread in Africa among savages a thousand miles in half a day. . . . Anyhow, that sort of thing *might* convince. To tell you the honest truth, Higginson, *your story doesn't.*"

Poor Mr. Higginson flushed. He did not like to be talked to like that. Babcock waited for his reply. It came at last, and came in the expected form.

"I can tell you, Babcock," began Higginson slowly, "something I 've told no one else. You 've driven me to do it. You know—you 've heard—that . . . that, well, that I *saw :* that I not only heard singing, but *saw ?* I saw a multitude of men—and women, Babcock."

He passed his hand over his face and wished himself well out of it—but Sin is a hard master.

"Well ? " asked Babcock, quite unchanged in face.

"Well," proceeded Professor Higginson, still more slowly, "this is what I have got to tell you. Many, all of those faces—and mind you they talked to me,"

Babcock, they *talked* to me" (the Professor was warming to his work)—" I didn't know.   But I knew one, Babcock," and here Higginson's voice fell (as his trick had grown to be during these recitals) to a deeper tone.   "Do you know who it was ?   .   .   . It was poor Morris ! "

Babcock rose again and came and stood over the wretched Philosopher.   The Philosopher looked up like a child, an erring child.

"Good   Heavens ! "   sighed   Babcock.   "What extraordinary ideas you have !   *That's* not what people notice.   Why, men can do that in their sleep."   Then with sudden vigour, "What *else* did you see, Higginson ?   Something you couldn't have known ?   Something nobody knew ? "

Professor Higginson thought.   Detailed imaginative fiction had never been in his line, though he had dealt in it pretty freely all that day.   He thought hard and confusedly ; but what he said at the end of the process was startling enough.

" Very well, Babcock, listen to this.   There was in that crowd a figure very different from the others— a mad figure, you will say.   Most mournful eyes, Babcock, and—well, it 's unpleasant, but it smelt of seaweed."

"Oh ! " said Babcock.   "Was it dressed ? "

Mr. Higginson thought a minute.

" Yes, it was *dressed*," he ventured, groping his way.   " Yes, it *was* dressed.   .   .   .   It was very *oddly* dressed.   You know . . . you see . . . it had dripping wet clothes on, dark blue.   But,

Babcock" (here Higginson had an inspiration, and
very proud of it he was), "*it had no arms!*"

"Oh," said Babcock, musing, "it had no arms."

There was a gap in their conversation, an end to
Babcock's pushing, an end to Higginson's lying. A
let up. An interval of repose.

It was Babcock who broke it.

"Well," he sighed, "I can't make head or tail of
all this, Higginson! Anyhow, I must be going.
It's interesting. I know you *think* you had these
experiences, but, frankly, all that kind of thing's
beyond me. I don't think it's *there*. I think it
floats in men's brains—false, like dreams," and he
got up to go.

But for the next half hour he was at the telephone
again, talking to London and to the Ancient
Aristocracy of Britain and to *The Howl*.

When he rose from the machine it was just eleven.
The Howl prints news up to two o'clock. Smart
Rag!

Next morning (Friday), when he came downstairs,
Professor Higginson received a slight but very unpleasant shock. It was a shock of a kind one does
not often receive.

Like all the rest of the world, Professor Higginson
read *The Howl* at breakfast. *The Howl* is very well
edited; it gives you your thrill in a short compass,
and every day has some new Portent to present.

That day the Portent was Sleeping Sickness on a
Huge Scale in London. Ten millionaires were down
with it and a politician was threatened. It wasn't

true, and there was a leader on it.   But true or false, it was of less consequence to Mr. Higginson than one fairly prominent but short item upon the front page. It was not the chief item on it ; the chief item was some rubbish about a man it called " the Kaiser." It was perhaps the second or the third piece of news in importance.

END OF A MYSTERIOUS CAREER.

NOBLEMAN   FOUND   DROWNED   ON BRETON COAST.

ROMANTIC STORY.

BREST, *Thursday, May 5th.*

Fishermen from the remote and old-world village of Karamel report a gruesome discovery upon their rock-bound coast.   The Count Michaelis de Quersaint, a well-known eccentric character in this district, evidently lost his life by shipwreck some few days ago in the neighbourhood.   It was the Count's habit to cruise up and down this coast during the summer months *incognito*, in a small ten-tonner, with a couple of men for crew, the unfortunate man having been born without arms, like a certain famous Irish landlord of the last generation, and being very sensitive upon the point.   The boat has not been found, but the bodies of three men, one of which is undoubtedly the Count, have been washed up on the rocks.   The features are unrecognisable, but there can be no doubt of Count Michaelis's identity. The corpse was clothed in the blue-serge yachting suit which the Count habitually wore on these expeditions, and the body was that of a man without arms. In the opinion of Dr. Relebecque, whom the Government has dispatched to Karamel, the disaster must have taken place about four days ago, and most probably during the gale of last Monday night.

The corpse was dressed in blue. It was drowned. It had no arms—a sort of monster.

Professor Higginson was unhappy, very unhappy indeed. He also felt sick.

Gusts of fear swept over his simple soul. There were moments when he almost smelt the pit, and he groaned in spirit.

So powerful was the effect upon him, that he was half persuaded of some connection between his foolish lie and doubtful superhuman powers. He didn't like it. It gave him a sense of possession. It left him not his own master.

He would not take up the paper again. He left it folded upon his table, and went out a little groggily to walk up the street to College and to take his class.

But when Professor Higginson appeared before his class he was nervously conscious that a great number of young eyes were watching him with quite as much amusement as interest.

Not that he was stared at. Provincials are too polite for that, and the earnest provincials who attend their Universities are perhaps the politest

class in England. But whenever he looked up from
his notes he met the glance shy and suddenly
withdrawn, now from the left, now from the right,
which told him that of the fifty or sixty students
before him not one was ignorant of the Great
Adventure.

His subject that morning was The Hypergraphical
Concatenation of the Major Sensory Criteria and
Psycho-hylomorphic Phenomena in their Relation
of the Subjective to the Objective Aspects of Reflex
Actions—a fascinating theme ! And one which,
upon any other day, he would have analysed with
the mouldy bravura that he had cultivated.

But that morning something flagged. The interest
of the class was elsewhere, and Professor Higginson
knew only too well where it was ! His misfortune
or accident was already so much public property
that the youths and maidens and the respectful
dependants and servitors of the University as well
were universally acquainted with it. He felt again
that touch of vanity in the midst of his embarrass-
ment !

The great clock of the University buildings boomed
out noon. He shut his notes, looked with his weary
eyes at the young faces before him, now lifted to his
own, and said—

" Next time we will take the Automatic Functions
of Guest and Bunny. It is new ground, and I think
it will interest you."

A timid, fair-haired girl to the rear of the left
centre asked whether they need buy the third

edition ; she only had the second. He said, full of thought for her purse, that there was no necessity to do such a thing, whereat the student added—

" But, Professor Higginson, it deals with the Subliminal Phenomena of a Loss of Mem ——"

" That 'll do ! That 'll do ! " cried Professor Higginson sharply.

He could have sworn that he heard a titter ! He looked up wearily at the window as his class tramped out.

It was raining.

When he had changed his Cap and Gown for the bowler hat, umbrella and mackintosh of his civilisation, he stepped out under the archway into the street, glad to be rid of his duties for the day, profoundly glad to be alone. He had fallen, as his habit was, into a conversation with himself, half aloud, happily oblivious of the suspicious glances of passers-by, which he would have imagined to be testimony to his unhappily growing fame, when he received a sharp blow upon the back from the open hand of some vigorous person, and turned round with an exclamation to see no less than Babcock—again.

Professor Higginson turned under his umbrella to catch that figure at his side, and saw beyond it a very different figure—a figure draped entirely in a long raincoat of some sort trailing almost to the ground ; peeping above the front of that coat was a clerical dog-collar, and above the clerical dog-collar a long face, the eyes of which always looked towards some spot far off.

"Well, Higginson," said Babcock, "you 've done it now."

"Done what ? " said Professor Higginson, knowing only too well what he had done.

"Made yourself famous," said George Babcock shortly.

"I don't know that ! " said Professor Higginson, and he nervously wondered whether the drip upon his back were from his own umbrella or his neighbour's. "Of course, a thing like that will be talked about."

"It 's what you said about the heavenly singing that did it," said George Babcock brutally ; and as he said it Professor Higginson, glancing at him sideways, saw a definite curl downwards upon the big, loose lips.

As they passed the door of the University Common Room, Babcock halted and said—

"Well, I 'm going in ! Are you coming with me, Higginson ? "

"No ! " said Professor Higginson, with singular determination.

"All right," said Babcock, not insisting. "Charles will see you home. I ought to have told you, this is my wife's brother, Charles ; he 's a parson," he added rudely, as though the external signs of that profession were absent. "You go with him, Charles. It 's on your way. Tell Clara I 'm coming. Back before one."

And George Babcock the strong pushed through the swing doors of the Club, and left his brother-in-law and his colleague in the rain outside.

Professor Higginson and the religious person walked for a few minutes in silence. For one thing the Philosopher did not know the name of the minister, and it was the minister who first broke that silence.

" You 've heard singing ! " he said abruptly, and as he said it he still stared in front of him, as at some distant point beyond this world, and steered himself by his great nose. He did not look at his companion, and he repeated in tones of subdued wonder, " You heard singing. I read it in the Ormeston paper to-day."

Professor Higginson had never in his life been rude to a man at the first meeting. He did not know how it was done.

" Yes," he said . . . " after a fashion."

" Ah ! " said the Reverend Charles, and they went on another fifty yards in silence through the rain. The streets were quite deserted.

Professor Higginson was appalled to find his companion's hand laid firmly upon his shoulder ; the other hand held the umbrella above. The parson looked immensely into his eyes.

" I wish I were you," he said, " or, rather, I don't wish I were you." Then he loosed hold, and they walked on together again.

Professor Higginson was profoundly uncomfortable. He was Professor of Subliminal Psychology, and far be it from him to fall into the vulgar errors of the materialist, but the man did seem to him a little cracked ; and when he whispered for the third time,

"You heard singing!" Professor Higginson was in that mood wherein weak men run. Now Professor Higginson prided himself that he was not a weak man.

The Reverend Charles began talking very loudly to himself, not in the half-tones of self-communion common to the academic temper, but quite out loud, almost as though he were preaching.

"Singing! 'Lovely chaunting voices, singing to the sound of harps, and in that light which dieth not, for they that stand in it are the inheritors of the world to come.' . . . That's from Pearson," he added abruptly, changing to a perfectly natural tone. "Do you know Pearson's work?"

"No," said Professor Higginson, immensely relieved at the change in the tone. "No, to tell the truth, I do not."

"He saw what you saw," said the Reverend gentleman, nodding gravely under his umbrella as he strode forward; "but he hadn't your chance of convincing the world. No!"

And here he shook his head as gravely as he had nodded it.

The rain still fell. The wet street still stretched out before them.

"It has been given to many men," began the Reverend Charles again in a totally different tone, this time the intellectual interrogative, "to see the hidden places, but your chance?"

Professor Higginson said nothing, he was beginning to feel uncomfortable again. He was not a materialist—what man of his great attainments could be ? But on the other hand there was such a thing as going too far in the other direction. Then he reasoned with himself. The Reverend Charles had no weapon. He, the Professor, was a tall man, and—hang it all ! he had no right to be certain that the man was mad.

They had come to Professor Higginson's door. There, in the pouring rain, Professor Higginson put in the latch key, opened the door, and asked in common courtesy whether his colleague's brother-in-law would come in.

His colleague's brother-in-law half shut a dripping umbrella, held out a huge and bony hand, fixed the embarrassed Don with luminous, distant eyes, grasped his nervously offered hand in return, and said sadly, with a world of meaning—

" No ! I will not come in ! I will leave you to Those Voices of the Great Peace ! "

Then it was that Professor Higginson noticed, standing in the mean little hall humbly enough, a mean little man, short, wearing a threadbare coat, and a drenched bowler hat.

" Professor Higginson," said this apparition gently, " Professor Higginson, I presume ? "

" What ? " snapped the Professor, still holding the Parson's hand, like the handle of a pump.

" May I see you a moment ? I represent *The Sunday Machine.*"

" No," thundered Professor Higginson, dropping the reverend hand in his excitement. " I 'm tired, it 's not lunch time yet, I don't know what you mean ! "

The little man was at once flabbergasted and hurt. The Reverend Charles smiled a cadaverous smile, but one as luminous as his eyes.

"May I supply the place?" he said in a voice that was musical in two tones.

He stood there winningly in the open doorway with his dripping umbrella and his huge, unoccupied right hand still held out.

The little reporter, not quite understanding what he should do, grasped that great hand, just as Professor Higginson had grasped it, and then stood helpless.

Professor Higginson was at the end of his patience. He said sharply—

"You must come again! You must come again! This isn't the moment."

In another minute he would have apologised for his abruptness, but the little journalist had pride and had already gone out, without an umbrella, thrusting his pathetic little note-book into his threadbare pocket; and the Reverend brother-in-law, after giving one great revealing look into the darkness of the hall, had gone out also. Professor Higginson heard the door slam behind him. His curiosity prompted him to gaze upon them out of a window. They were going off together through the rain, into the heart of the town, and it seemed to the Philosopher that the Parson was more animated than before. He turned to his companion continually, and his gestures were broad. More fame was brewing!

All that Friday afternoon he kept his room. He forbade Mrs. Randle to admit a soul. He went to bed early and slept ill. The wages of sin is death.

Professor Higginson came down next morning in a very miserable mood. A vast pile of letters stood beside his plate, and there also he saw *The Howl*, folded, keeping its dreadful secret—he was sure it had one for him.

The sheet, with its harmless outer cover, its advertisements of patent poisons and its bold title menaced him. It fascinated him too. He hesitated, reached for it, opened it, and the blow fell.

To his horror, there stared him in the face two great lines—nay, three, of huge block headline type, counting more in the front page of that day than the sleeping sickness, than the might of Germany, or the turpitude of Kalmazoo.

They ran thus—

EVIDENCE OF A FUTURE LIFE!

REVELATIONS OF A GREAT PSYCHOLOGIST.

PROFESSOR HIGGINSON TESTIFIES TO SUPERNATURAL EXPERIENCES.

RECOGNITION OF THE DEAD.

There are parts of the body that grow cold under excitement of an unpleasant type. Among these may be noted the forehead, certain muscles upon either side of the vertebræ, and the region of the knees.

Had Professor Higginson been free to note these interesting phenomena proceeding in his own person, it might have been of advantage to science.   All he knew was that he felt extremely ill.   He pushed his breakfast plate away from him, folded the paper into two, rose from the table, and stood bending over the mantelpiece with his head upon his hand.   Then he mastered himself, sat down, and began to read this—

Ormeston, *May 5th,* Friday.

(From our Special Correspondent.)

I am authorised to publish an experience altogether unique which has befallen one of the most respected members of the Guelph University, Ormeston, and one, moreover, whose peculiar functions at the University give him an unchallenged authority on the matter in question.
Professor Higginson, who holds the Chair of Subliminal Psychology in the University, is in the possession, through a recent experience, of undoubted proofs of the existence of the soul of beings of human origin in a state of consciousness of other than terrestrial conditions.

What followed, and what his pained eyes most wearily discerned, was the nature of the proof : the impossibility that anyone in Ormeston should have heard of that drowned thing upon the French coast ; the hour in which Professor Higginson had told a

colleague of the experience—fully four hours before
the discovery itself was made—five hours before the
belated Breton telegram had reached *The Howl*
from its Paris office. The whole thing was a convincing chain. And with that dreadful knowledge
men have that they are in for it, Professor Higginson
laid the paper down, and wondered how much must
be endured before the blessed touch of death.

CHAPTER VIII

In which Professor Higginson gets those sweets by the wagon-load, and also hears how Men are Made

PROFESSOR HIGGINSON stared at the pile of letters. He remembered that it was a Saturday—a free day! He groaned at such freedom.

Fame is like the trumpet she bears. The trumpet has for the civilian an exhilarating sound; for the house near barracks, too familiar with it, a mechanical one; for the mounted trooper at reveillée it has nothing but a hideous blare.

Fame had come to Professor Higginson under her less pleasing aspect. He marvelled that so much fame had already risen. He trembled at what *The Howl* might now raise. A paltry lapse of memory! A thing that might happen to anyone! And now all this!

Professor Higginson had under-estimated his position in the scientific world of guess-work.

There are not many Professors of Psychology. Only three have written books. That his own should have been translated into several languages had in the past given him pleasure, for he was a provincial man, and in that curious mixture which makes your academic fellow the funny thing he is, the enormity of false pride jostles a very real simplicity.

He opened one letter, then another, then another : he intended to answer each laboriously at some length with his own hand. He had said nothing of confidence or of privacy to any man, and these letters were the firstfruits of what might be to come !

The Howl is read by all England before nine. There is a post comes into Ormeston at three in the afternoon. By that post, amid a mass of material which it appalled him to observe, and which included every kind of advertisement from every sort of tout, there was shot at the Philosopher over two hundred letters of more material kind.

He purposed an attempt to answer even these in as much detail as his first batch and with his own hand. His Great Adventure was becoming a matter of appreciable interest to himself, and half to conquer, in some moments, his anxiety and dread. There came interludes—as he sat that afternoon opening envelope after envelope, and scribbling notes for replies—when he really felt as though what he were writing was true, and could describe with glowing precision all that strange psychic phase in which the Sub-Conscious self kicks up its heels and gambols at random unrestrained by the burden of objectivity.

Two letters in particular he wrote with the utmost care. One to a Cabinet Minister—an inveterate meddler who dabbled in such things in the intervals of his enormous occupations — the other to an ex-Cabinet Minister—another inveterate meddler who also dabbled in such things in the intervals of his.

Professor Higginson had never written to such great men before.. He worked really hard, and he composed two masterpieces. Upon the addressing of his first ten envelopes he spent the best part of twenty minutes with books of reference at his side. He wrote courteously and at enormous length to a Great Lady whose coronet stood out upon the paper like a mountain, and whose signature he could yet hardly accept as real, so tremendous a thing did it seem to him that such an one as She should have entered his life.

He wrote in extraordinary French to the great Specialist at Nancy who had written to him in English. He wrote in English to the great Specialist of Leipsic who had written to him in a German he did not understand, but whose signature and European name warranted the nature of the reply. So passed all Saturday's leisure.

Then came Sunday morning—and a perfect ocean of post !

It was a mass of correspondence which no two secretaries could have dealt with in thirty-six hours, and which he left hopelessly upon his table until some expert friend might tell him how such heaps were cleared.

His immense work of the day and of the night before in answering the Great had left him weary and already disgusted with his new public position. His terrors returned.

He had overstrained himself. The room was blurred before him. He rose from his breakfast and thought to take the air—but the empty Sabbath streets brought him no relief.

The Sunday Popular Papers were hot on his trail. Their great flaring placards stood outside the news shops.

" Is there a Heaven ? " in letters a foot long, and underneath, " Professor Higginson says ' Yes,' " almost knocked him down as they stared at him from one hoarding. In the loud bill outside a chapel he saw his name set forth as the " subject of the discourse," and before he could snatch away his eyes he had caught the phrase : " The First Witness." All were welcome. . . . *He* was the First Witness ! . . . Oh, God !

He could not pursue his walk. He felt (quite unnecessarily) that the mass of the people whom he passed noted him, and spoke of him among themselves as the Author of the Great Revelation. He wished again for the hundredth time that he had never meddled with a lie. Then Satan jerked the bit : Professor Higginson remembered what the truth would have brought him ; he thought of the dock. And then he ceased to wish for anything at all.

Just as he was turning back from that *via dolorosa* of newspaper placards and sermon-notices in the public street, he remembered the mass of correspondence, and at that moment Heaven sent him a friend —it was Babcock. The set face and hard, bepuffed eyes seemed to shine on him like the light of doom ;

the great loose mouth seemed eager and hungry to devour a victim of such eminence.

Professor Higginson did not let him take the offensive.

" Babcock," he almost shouted in his agony, " you know about letters and things ? "

Babcock never looked bewildered. He nodded his head determinedly and said—

" Go on."

" Well," continued Professor Higginson, fiercely determined that the great subject should not turn up, and talking as though by steam, " letters, you know about letters, letters, hundreds and hundreds of them. Must deal with them, must deal with them this morning—now ! " he almost screamed.

The heavy Babcock rapidly diagnosed the case within his mind. He forbore to exasperate the patient.

" That 's all right," he said about as soothingly as ogres can. " That 's all right. What you want is a shorthand writer."

" Two ! " shouted Higginson, still dragging his companion along.

But the heavy Babcock had organising power.

" What 's the good of two ? " he said contemptuously. " You haven't got two mouths—nor two brains either," he added unnecessarily.

" I want help ! " said Professor Higginson wildly. " Help ! "

" What you want," said the heavy Babcock, with a solid mental grip that mastered his victim, " is someone to open all those letters, and sort 'em out, one from the other, and see what ought to be said, eh ?   Kind of thing that ought to be said.   Got a telephone ? "

"No—yes—no," said Professor Higginson as he reached his door.

"You ought to have—a man of your position," said Babcock. They had reached the door. "I 'll come in and help you," he added.

He did so.   He set to work at once did Babcock —strongly and well,   He reproved his unhappy colleague again for not having a telephone, sent out a servant in a cab with the address of a shorthand writer and of a typist, newspaper people obtainable of a Sunday, and he ordered a machine.   Then he proceeded with tremendous rapidity to slice open the great heap of envelopes with a butter knife.

He sorted out their contents at a pace that appalled and yet fascinated the Professor of Psychology.   By the time the assistants had come he had them in four heaps :—

        (1) Big-Wigs,
        (2) Money,
        (3) Refusals, and
        (4) (largest of all) Trash.

Then did he take it upon himself without leave to call out to the shorthand writer—

"First sentence—I hope you will excuse my dictating this letter—' The pressure of my correspondence during the last few days has been as you may imagine far too great, etc., etc.' "

It was a noble, rotund, convenient sentence. It had done work in its time. Higginson listened, more fascinated than ever.

"Thirty copies of that, please," said Babcock sharply. Then he condescended to explain.

"That 'll come after the ' Dear Sir or Madam.' "

Higginson nodded and added faintly—

"Or ' My Lady,' or whatever it may be."

"Yes," said Babcock, suddenly glancing at him with a gimlet look, "after the opening thing whatever it is, ' My Lord Duke, or My Lord Cardinal, Excellence, or My Lord Hell-to-Pay.' "

He busied himself again with the papers.

"Those," he said, shuffling rapidly a body of over forty and suddenly tearing them across, ."that 's trash ; principally lunatics. I can' tell 'em by the hand."

Higginson gazed on helplessly ; he thought such destruction imprudent, but he said nothing.

"These," went on Babcock, groaning with intelligent interest, and licking his forefinger to deal with the papers, "these are refusals."

He turned leaf after leaf as though he were counting Bank Notes, and decided upon the lot.

"Yes ; all refusals."

"May I look ? " said Professor Higginson a little weakly.

"Yes, if you like," said Babcock, throwing over the pile without looking up, and turning to the next.

The Professor discovered that his colleague was right enough. They were invitations all of them,

and not invitations· to accept. Over a third were
from money-lenders. He made a plaintive appeal
to keep certain of these last, whose gorgeous crests,
ancient names, and scented paper fascinated him.
Babcock merely grunted and said, putting his hand
upon another much smaller pile—

"These are *money*, Higginson, *money*."

He read them out. An offer to write for a
magazine ; a much more lucrative offer to write for
The Only Daily Paper—but to write exclusively—
and so forth.

"That 's the one to take," said Babcock, he pulled
out a note with an American heading, ticked it,
and tossing it to the Professor, said—

"Shall I answer it for you ? "

"No," said Higginson, trying to be firm.

"Oh, very well then," said Babcock, "dictate it
yourself."

And the Professor with infinite verbiage gratefully
accepted an exclusive article of three thousand
words for the sum of £250.

It was the turn of the Big-Wigs, and the learned
Babcock with unerring eye skipped an actor and a
Duchess of equal prominence, and fished out The
Great Invitation.

It was the first document upon which he had
condescended to linger, and though it was short, he
spent some moments over it. His face grew grave.

"That 's a big thing ! " he said solemnly, handing
it over almost with reverence to the Professor of
Psychology.

The Professor read a good London address simply stamped upon a good piece of note paper. He saw a signature, "Leonard Barclay," which he vaguely remembered in some connection or other. He read an invitation to deliver an address for the Research Club upon any day he might choose, but if possible during the next week. The Research Club would take for the occasion the large room at Gorton's. That was all.

"Lucky beast!" murmured Babcock, not quite loud enough for the typist to hear, as he fixed the reading Higginson with his eye.

The reading Higginson laid down the letter, nodded inanely, and said—

"Well, ought I to take that, Babcock? Who *are* the Research Club?"

"Who are the Research Club? Wuff! What a man! They *make* men!" said Babcock bitterly, "that 's what they are! Do you mean to say you don't *know?*" he went on, leaning over and talking earnestly in a low tone. "Do you mean to say you haven't *heard* of the Research Club?"

"Somewhere, I dare say," said Professor Higginson confusedly.

But he hadn't. It was a great moment for Babcock. He had not been among the "nuts" for nothing.

"Come," said he, like a man who is leading up to a great business, "you know who Leonard Barclay is?"

"No—yes," said Professor Higginson.

"Just like your telephone," sneered Babcock. "You *don't* know. Well, I'll tell you. Leonard Barclay's the private secretary of Mrs. Camp, and *he's* the man who started the Connoisseurs in Bond Street, and who wrote the book about Colombo. *Now* do you understand?"

Professor Higginson dared not say he didn't. But he still looked helpless.

"Good God, man!" Babcock went at him again, "*he's in the very middle of it.* I've known invitations from the R.C. sent by lots of people, but never by *him!*"

"Oh!" said Higginson, with an appearance of comprehension, though in truth the mysteries of our plutocracy were for him mysteries indeed. "Is he in Parliament?"

"Parliament!" sneered Babcock. "You'll be asking me if he's the Lord Mayor next. He's Leonard Barclay. . . . Oh, curse it! He's *it!* He's in the middle of the pudding. Why, man alive, he made" (and Babcock with glorious indiscretion quoted right off the reel) "the Under-Secretary for the Post Office, the General in command of the 5th Army Corps, the Permanent Commissioner of Fine Arts, and a Bishop—a Bishop who really counted."

He paused for breath, and he emphasised his words slowly as he leant back again.

"Do you know, Higginson, that Leonard Barclay was the man who let Lord Cowfold leave the country?"

"What!" said the astonished and provincial Professor. "What do you mean? . . . Lord Cowfold?—why, he was at Ormeston only last May opening the Bulldog Club."

"Well, he's in Assisi now," said Babcock grimly, "Assisi in Italy; and he can thank Leonard Barclay that he's not in Dartmoor—Dartmoor in Devonshire. Lord, man, you're in luck!"

"But I don't understand," began Professor Higginson, and then he was silent.

"Well, then, I'll tell you," said Babcock, gloating in triumph, "though it's difficult to believe you! The Research Club is Bakewell and the Prime Minister and Fittleworth and Capley and about twenty more like that, and when you talk before it, you don't *only* talk before it, Higginson, you talk before anything that counts in Europe and happens to be in England at the time."

"But I never heard of it," said his colleague impotently, with the feeling as he said it that *that* was no great proof of anything.

"No," answered Babcock grimly, "one doesn't always hear of those things."

He jotted down a few words in pencil on a bit of paper and shoved it over to the Professor.

"There," he said, "copy that out in your own hand. I wouldn't type-write a thing of that sort if I were you—and write it on the University paper."

Professor Higginson peered at the note and read—

" My dear Mr. Barclay,

"I shall really be very happy.   I think Wednesday
a very good night.   Shall we call it Wednesday?
Unless I hear from you I shall take it for granted;
and at Gorton's.   The usual hour, I suppose?"

Professor Higginson gasped.

"But isn't that very familiar, Babcock," he said
doubtfully.

"Yes, it is," said Babcock, "that's the point."

"And I don't know the hour," said Higginson,
still hesitating.

"But I do," said Babcock.   "It's half-past five.
Listen, Higginson, and don't be a fool.   That's
how men are *made* in this country.   Do as I tell
you."

Professor Higginson, wondering vaguely how he
could be "made," and what happened when a man
was so dealt with by those that govern us, took a
sheet of the University paper, and wrote out carefully
that horribly familiar note.   He hesitated at the
superscription.

"What is he?" he asked.

"Who?" said Babcock.

"Why, this Mr. ——, this something Barclay."

"You've got it there, you fool," said Babcock
without courtesy.   "Leonard Barclay, Leonard
Barclay, Esq.   Simple enough, isn't it?"

"I thought," murmured Professor Higginson,
"I didn't know—er it was possible that he might
have had a ——"

" Father ? " blurted out Babcock. " Not that I know of. No one knows where he comes from, 'xcept Mrs. Camp, and *she* comes from Chicago."

With which words Babcock, the fallen angel, stared before him in reverie, and saw rising upon the background of that dull provincial room all his old lost paradise : the glories of the Merschauer's house in Capon Street, and the big day at Cowfold House, and the crowds, and the lights that surround our masters and his.

Thus it was that there fell upon this worthy, stilted and hitherto rather obscure provincial pedant the Great Chance of English life : to receive a note from the private secretary of the widow of Mr. Camp, of Chicago, and to speak before the Research Club, where, as it seems, Men are Made !

CHAPTER IX

In which the Green Overcoat begins to assert itself

" AND what," say you (very properly), " what of the Green Overcoat all this time ? After all, it is the title of the book, and I am entitled to hear more about the title. I did not get this book to hear all about a hotch-potch of human beings, I got it to read about the Green Overcoat. What of the Green Overcoat ? "

Softly ! I bear it in mind.

The adventures of the Green Overcoat throughout those days, when it had taken vengeance upon the human beings who had separated it from its beloved master, may be simply told.

The police in this country know from hour to hour what we do and how we do it ; if they were better educated, they would even be able to know why we do it. The travels of any object not honestly come by—if it remain at least in the hands of the poor—may be traced in good time (by the conscientious historian who has access to Scotland Yard) as unerringly as a North Hants fox who, before entertaining the hunt, has been kept in a motor pit for three days.

When Professor Higginson had charged the Man

with the Broken Nose with the task of restoring
the Green Overcoat to its owner, and had generously
prepaid the proletarian for his services upon that
occasion, I regret to say that the citizen entrusted
with the fulfilment of such a duty most shamefully
neglected it.

He did indeed proceed a certain distance in the
direction of Crampton Park under the open morning
sun, whistling as he went, with the object of convincing his probably suspicious and certainly jealous
comrades in the Shelter of his integrity.   But when
he had got to cover behind a row of cottages, the
strange action to which he descended betrayed
the baseness of his moral standard.

He no longer continued in the direction of
Crampton Park : not he ! He dodged at a brisk
pace with the heavy thing upon his arm, zigzagging
right and left through the streets of the slum-suburb,
and soon left the houses for a deserted field which a
blank wall hid from neighbouring windows, and to
which I must suppose that he had upon various
occasions betaken himself when he desired privacy
in some adventure.

Seated upon a rubbish heap which adorned that
plot of ground, the Man with the Broken Nose first
very carefully felt in either pocket of the bargain,
and found nothing but a cheque book.

He pulled it out and held it hesitatingly for a few
moments in his stubby right hand.

The Man with the Broken Nose was not without
his superstitions—superstitions common, I fear, to

his class—and one of these was Cheque Books. He knew indeed that with a Cheque Book great things could be done, but he knew not how. He had not possession of the magic password, or of the trick whereby this powerful instrument governs the modern world. He wondered for a moment a little thickly in his early morning mind whether a price were given for such things. For himself he regretfully concluded it was a mystery. He put it back. But even as he did so something in the heap of rubbish gave way, he slipped, and was suddenly acutely conscious of a warm wet feeling in his right calf : it came from a broken bottle.

His leg in the slipping of the rubble had met the glass, and the glass had won ; nor did that great Green Overcoat, all sumptuously lined with fur, give a hint of its dread amusement.

The blood was pouring severely from the wound. The Man with the Broken Nose had suffered accidents before ; he knew that this might be serious. He lifted his trouser leg, saw the bad gash, and for a moment gently pressed the lips of the wound together.

" It 's a jedgment ! " he said. " It 's a jedgment ! " he repeated to himself.

But even so manifest a sign from On High would not deter him from his purpose. He tore from his shirt a strip wherewith to bind his leg, and limped with increasing pain back towards the streets of the town.

He was seeking a house not unknown to him, for it was a place where those who have few friends can always find a friend, the residence of a Mr. Montague, Financier and Master of those mean streets; and as he limped, carrying his booty upon his arm, he cursed.

The morning sun brought him no gladness. The Green Overcoat seemed heavier and heavier with every yard of his way, until at last he stood before a house like any other of those unhappy little houses wherein our industrial cities rot, save that its glass was a little dirtier, its doorstep more neglected, its paint more faded than that of its neighbours.

For a moment the Man with the Broken Nose hesitated. The day was extremely young. Mr. Montague might not care to be aroused. It was important for him and for many like him that he should keep Mr. Montague's good will. Then he remembered that in a little time the Knocker-up would come his rounds, and that that wretched street of slaves would wake to work for the rich in the city.

The thought decided him. He rapped gently with his knuckles on the ground floor window. There was no response. He rapped a second time. A terse but unpleasant oath assured him that he had aroused whoever slept therein. A minute or two later he heard shuffling slippers moving cautiously across the passage. The door was opened a crack, and a very short man, very old, hump-backed one would almost say, with a beard of prodigious growth and beastliness tucked into a dressing-gown more greasy than the beard, stood in the darkness behind the half-open door.

"I do 'umbly beg pardon," began the Man with

the Broken Nose, making of the Green Overcoat a sort of shield and offering at once. "I do 'umbly beg pardon, Mr. Montague, but I thought —— "

"Curth what you thought!" said the bearer of that ancient crusading name, in a voice so husky it could hardly be heard. "Curth what you thought! Come in!"

The Man with the Broken Nose slipped in with something of the carriage that a poor trapper might show who should take refuge from a bear in the lair of a snake.

"I 'umbly beg pardon," he began again in the darkness of the passage, and the old bearded apparition with the crusading name answered—

"Shut your mouth!"

The Man with the Broken Nose obeyed.

The cautious, shuffling slippers led the way. A match was struck. The little dangerous figure reached up on tip-toe and lit a flaring unprotected gas-jet. The only window giving upon that passage was boarded.

"Take it inter the light, Mr. Montague, take it inter the light!" said the visitor eagerly, making as though to open the door of a further room which would be flooded with the morning sun.

His hand was upon the latch. With a curious, hardly audible snarl, Mr. Montague caught that hand a sharp blow on the wrist, and it said much for Mr. Montague's high standing with the Ormeston poor that the Man with the Broken Nose took no offence.

Under the flaring gas-jet Mr. Montague was turning the Green Overcoat over and over again.

"Give yer a quid," he said after about three minutes of close inspection.

"Why, Mr. Montague, sir !" the other had just begun, when he heard a hiss which formed the words, "Wish you may die !" and felt upon his shoulder the grip that was not like the grip of a human hand, but like the grip of a talon.

The Man with the Broken Nose was not prepared to argue. There had been one or two things in his full and varied life which if Mr. Montague had mentioned them even in a whisper would have made him less inclined to argue still, and he knew that Mr. Montague had a way of whispering sometimes into the ear of Memory things which a better breeding would have respected.

Mr. Montague knew the value of time. Far up the line of streets the first strokes of the Knocker-up were heard.

The Man with the Broken Nose found himself a moment later standing in the street with one sovereign in his hand for a twenty-guinea garment, and looking at the shut door and the meaningless, dirty windows which contained his prize.

He wished the new owner joy in Hell, he wished it aloud with that amazing bitterness which the poor of our great cities distil more copiously than any men on earth : for of all men upon all the earth they are the most miserable.

He took out the sovereign he had just received,

and his mood changed. He spat on it for luck. He felt himself going curiously lightly, and then he remembered of what a burden he was rid. He walked without difficulty, and only in a hundred yards or two did he remember his wound. It seemed to have healed quickly. It had not opened. He almost felt as though it were healing—and now I am concerned with him no more. The Green Overcoat is out of his keeping, and has no intention of returning to it.

But in the filthy little room of that filthy little house the filthy little bearer of the old crusading name, Mr. Montague, sat huddled upon his bed—a bed he made himself, or rather left unmade from week to week—and examined carefully upon his knee the fur, the cloth, the make of the gorgeous apparel.

He smiled, and as he smiled he sneered. For God had so made Mr. Montague that sneering and smiling were with him one thing.

There was value in that piece of cloth upon his knee, but it was of two kinds : value to anyone who would buy, more value, perhaps, to some owner that would recover. He considered either chance, and even as he considered them and sat staring at the expanse of Green Cloth an odd thing happened ; not in the external world, nor within the walls of that room, but within the old man's mind. He thought suddenly of Death !

A tremor passed over the whole surface of his skin, downwards from his neck to his feet. He

coughed and spat—clear of the Green Overcoat—
upon the floor ; and he cursed for a moment in a
language that was not English. Then the thought
passed as suddenly as it had come, and he was himself
again, but the weaker for that moment. His hand
trembled as he set it to do what every hand appeared
so prone to do when the Green Overcoat came near
it. He put' that trembling hand into the left-hand
pocket and found nothing. He had expected as
much. Was it likely that his visitor would have
left anything ? For form's sake he put it into the
right-hand pocket in turn ; and thence, to his
amazement, he drew out the Cheque Book.

He looked at it stupidly for a moment, not understanding how such a prize should conceivably have
been abandoned. Then he smiled again that not
cheerful smile, and slowly consulted the name of the
bank and of the owner, and the counterfoils one by
one.

The sums that stood therein called to him like
great heralds ; they made his puny old chest heave
and certain muscles in him grow rigid.

He was in the midst of the tale when his whole
being fainted within him, as it were—stopped dead
at the noise of a violent rain of blows upon his outer
door.

CHAPTER X

In which a Descendant of the Crusaders refuses to harbour stolen goods

FOR just that time—how long it is or how short no man who has felt it can tell—for just that time it takes the body to recover itself from a halt of the blood, the old man sat immovable, his eyes unnaturally bright and unwinking like a bird's.

Then motion returned to him, and it was a motion as rapid as a lizard's.

His greasy old dressing-gown was off. The ample, the substantial, the English Green Overcoat was on that miserable, shrivelled form of the old man with the crusading name. His sticks of arms were struggling wildly into the massive sleeves, when that thundering at the door came again, and with it a loud, peremptory order in a voice which he knew.

Mr. Montague coaxed on, with quite other gestures, over the overcoat and like a skin, that vast, greasy dressing-gown wherein for so many years he had shuffled across the lonely floors of his four-room house. He was in the passage, and was trying to shout, forcing his voice huskily—

" You 'll break the door ! You 'll break the door ! "

He opened it. Two men were outside whom he knew. Each was burly and strong. Each carried

146

upon a well-fed body a large, sufficient, beefy face.
Each had the bearing of a trained, drilled man. The
one who stood somewhat forward as the superior
had something approaching to kindness in his
intelligent eyes, and both had the eyes of brave
men—though not of loyal ones.

"Well, Sammy?" said the one in command.

"Oh, Mr. Ferguson! Mr. Ferguson!" came in
Mr. Montague's half-voice.

"Well, Sammy," said Mr. Ferguson again, "you
nearly lost some of your paint that time! You
weren't asleep, Sam," he said, winking; "you ——'s
never are! I believe you sleep dinner-time, like the
owls."

The inferior of the two visitors grinned as in duty
bound at the excellent joke. Mr. Montague smiled
with the smile of an aged idol.

"Mr. Ferguson! Mr. Ferguson!" he rasped in
that half-voice of his, "yer will have yer fun!"

He led the two big men in. It was curious to note
how these Englishmen of the Midlands showed a sort
of deference in their gesture, an old inherited thing,
as they entered another man's house. The lesser of
them made to wipe his boots, but there was no mat.
Mr. Montague sniffed and smiled or sneered, or
sneered and smiled.

"Mister," he said to the second of the two, "I don't
know yer name?"

He did not say this in a very pleasant way.

"Never mind, Samuel," said Mr. Ferguson heartily,
"he's only just joined the force. You'll know him

soon enough." And he laughed out loud in a manner very different from Mr. Montague's.

"And now then, Samuel," he added, "we haven't much time to lose."

He pulled himself up (he had been a soldier) and he led the way mechanically to the second little ground-floor room at the back, which he had visited often and often before in his capacity of that member of the Ormeston police who best knew and could best deal with receivers. Mr. Ferguson was, you see, the providence of these financiers, managing them, saving them — punishing them reluctantly when it was absolutely necessary, but generally keeping them (as a matter of policy) upon a string, and through them controlling his knowledge of all the avenues by which the more adventurous of the poor played Tom Tiddler's ground upon the frills of the propertied classes.

Mr. Montague shuffled as he had shuffled so often before, he shuffled cautiously after the burly man. As he shuffled he protested for the mere sake of ritual, and chuckled the while a little to himself as though he were thinking aloud—

"Me! Me of all men! S'help!"

Mr. Ferguson went in. There was not much in the place. Five or six articles of furniture recently sold at an auction, which the policeman recognised as being legally acquired ; an exceedingly dirty oil-picture in an even dirtier frame, which his innocent eyes thought might be an old master. He kicked it with his foot.

"What 's that ? " he said.

Mr. Montague was alarmed.

"Don't yer kick that with your foot now ; come, don't yer ! " he whispered through his defective throat imploringly. "Don't yer there ! It 's right as Rechts. May I die ! 'Tis surely."

He looked up anxiously, and put a protecting hand upon it.

The policeman moved it roughly forward and saw a label upon the back. He remembered the sale and let it go again.

" Yes," he said, " that 's all right, Samuel."

A dusty book, the binding half torn off of it, lay upon a shelf, worthless if anything was. Mr. Ferguson took it up mechanically, hardly knowing what he was at ; but as he did so he heard an almost imperceptible sound coming from the old receiver's mouth, a sort of gasp. It was a sound that betrayed anxiety, and it warned him. He picked up that book and opened it. It was a copy of Halidon's *History of Ormeston*. He turned the leaves mechanically, and was banging it down again, when there appeared a thing unusual in the leaves of such a book—a corner of much whiter paper, crinkly and crisp, unmistakable. Mr. Ferguson pulled out a five-pound note.

"Wish I may ——" began the husky old voice almost inaudibly, and then ceased.

Mr. Ferguson turned round and winked enormously.

"Contrariwise, Sammy ! Wish you *mayn't !* Long life to you," he said.

He turned again to the book, carefully turned its

leaves, picked out one by one ten five-pound notes, shook it roughly upside down, and concluded there were no more.

" Artful ! " he said admiringly.

Mr. Montague knew all the ropes.

" I can tell yer, bright ! " he whispered eagerly.

" Ah, I know you would ! " said the big Midlander with a good-humoured laugh. " Not flash goods are they ? "

" No, Mr. Ferguson, no," came the whisper again, pathetically eager, " nor my own savings neither. I won't lie to yer, Mr. Ferguson, sir ! I won't ! Bright ! I did it t' oblige a widder ! "

" I understand," said Mr. Ferguson genially, putting a reassuring hand upon Mr. Montague's shoulder. " Bless you ! We wouldn't lose you, Sam, not for di'monds, we wouldn't ! But we 're bound to go to the bank, you know," he added in his duty tone, " and we 're bound to prosecute if we find who did the pinching ! "

Mr. Montague was reassured.

" I am a sort of banker, Mr. Ferguson," he whispered sadly. " I did truly do it t' oblige."

" We know, Sammy," said the big man, winking again ponderously, " that 's a by-blow ! That 's a come-by-chance ! You shan't suffer for it, only if we find that widow . . ."

Mr. Montague was reassured and smiled that smile, and the inferior policeman grinned also an honest grin. He was there to learn the tricks of the trade, and he only half understood them.

"Look here, Samuel," said the big man, turning round suddenly and squarely, "we're not after that, you know! We're not after a general rummage either this time." (He carefully folded, tied up, and pocketed the bank-notes as he spoke, taking their numbers one by one with a pencil upon his pocket-book.) "We're after something pertickler. Now you'll know if anyone does, and no harm'll come to you, Samuel, so think! Ye've heard o' Mr. Brassington?"

Mr. Montague was about to shake his head, when he suddenly remembered that everyone in Ormeston knew Mr. Brassington, and instead of shaking his head he nodded it—abstractedly. All his narrow, keen mind was full of the name Brassington, which he had seen written so bold and large upon the cover of the rich cheque book that warmed with a heavenly glow a certain pocket just beneath his dressing-gown upon the right-hand side.

Mr. Ferguson said no more, but led the way back ponderously into the dirty little bedroom. He sat down upon the only rickety chair, his inferior standing, almost at attention, feeling there was something solemn about the moment. Mr. Montague sat upon the dirty little huddled bed, and watched the two Englishmen with weary unconcern.

"Samuel," said Mr. Ferguson in a new and graver tone, "*you* know all the lays and the lags about here, don't you?"

Mr. Montague did not reply; he tried to begin to smile, but stopped the smile with a cough.

"Well, now, there's a Green Overcoat of Mr. Brassington's. Maybe you know it. Most do. He's allus in it."

Mr. Montague shook his head in some despair, and continued to listen.

"Anyhow, it's not here," continued Mr. Ferguson. "You wouldn't fake it, Sammy ; it's not worth it, otherwise we'd have looked upstairs," he added knowingly.

Mr. Montague smiled in reply, a genuine smile. The policemen knew when to go upstairs and when not.

"It's not worth twenty quid," went on Mr. Ferguson earnestly, "if you should see it. It's not worth" (he sought in his mind for a comparison) "blarst me ! it's not worth six months," he concluded with emphasis.

Mr. Montague accompanied this speech by a continued slow shaking of the head and an inverted vague look in his little bright eyes, as though he were seeking for some memory of the thing—some glimpse of it within his wide circle of acquaintances.

"It's not here," said Mr. Ferguson for the last time, rising, "I can see that, and I know ye, but if ye should see anything of it ——"

The old man's whisper was close to the policeman's ear, for he also had risen. It came reassuring and husky.

"I know which ways I lies abed !" he said. Then he winked, sharply, like a bird, and Mr. Ferguson was thoroughly content.

One last piece of ritual had to be gone through before this cog in our vast and admirable administrative system had ground through and done its work. The little old bearded man shuffled to a corner and brought out a bottle and three glasses. He poured out generously into theirs, slightly into his, and they all three—the two Englishmen and the Crusader—drank together.

Mr. Montague had seen the inside of a prison once —it was thirty years before, and for a few weeks only. He was new to this country then. Mr. Ferguson knew that Mr. Montague cherished no passionate desire to see those sights again, and the big policeman went out into the morning sun and walked off with his subordinate down the street. They walked in those absurd twin suits of dittoes and regulation boots, which, when the Police go out in civilian disguise, shriek " The Force ! The Force ! " to all the poor before whom the vision passes.

*   *   *   *   *

Mr. Montague from within his little room peered through the curtains.

His face was no longer the same. It was the face of a man younger and yet more evil.

He slipped off his greasy lizard-skin of a dressing-gown as though he were preparing deliberately for some evil deed. He tore and struggled himself out of that maleficent green, fur-lined cloth ; he spat on it ; then he rubbed clean the place where he had spat, and cursed it lengthily and with a nasty voice in a language that is not ours. Now and then his talons of hands made as though to tear the fabric. He snarled at it and clawed at it twice—but he would not damage it ; it would fetch twenty pounds.

He sat, a skeleton effigy, with his too-large, bearded head, draped only in the aged night-shirt of his solitude, and, by I know not what disastrous processes of the mind, now shrank from, now turned towards the pieces of green cloth lying squat on the bed as though it had been a living thing. Then he began muttering about his ten five-pound notes. He gave them names, turning them into strange foreign money. There was more in the bank. Oh, there was more ! But all the days he had kept them hidden—waiting for the thing to blow over ! And how cheap he had bought that paper, and how well he thought to have hidden it ; what a certain scheme against curious eyes ! Those five flimsy papers between the leaves of such a book, and all those regular visits of the Force, regular as the month came round, and never such a thing as a loss before !

In his old head, so clear, so narrow and so keen, there ran in spite of reason the craft of dead centuries and tales of demons inhabiting human things. He had not eaten. He had been awakened too early from sleep. He had suffered agony and loss. It was the fault of the Green Overcoat ! of the accursed thing before him ! But that thing was worth twenty pounds.

For a moment he fingered (and felt sacrilegious as he did so) the right-hand pocket. He touched within it the cheque book. There arose in him almost simultaneously a vision of what one could do with the cheque book of a really wealthy man, a man with a large balance for his private whims, a man known to be generously careless ; and as he had that vision there came with it another vision—the vision of the inside of a British prison, the nearest thing to Hell which God permits on earth.

It was the second vision that conquered. The old man drew his fingers from that cheque book as a man in cold weather draws his fingers reluctantly from the fire.

Then, with sudden haste, and muttering all the while those curious curses in a tongue which is not ours, he folded the thing together, drew from beneath the ramshackle bed (where there was a great store of it) a large sheet of dirty and thick paper, and one of many lengths of string that there lay rolled.

He made a bundle of the Green Overcoat, hurriedly, misshapenly. He drew on a pair of trousers, covered his upper body with a great ulster, most unsuitable to the season, groped for a round hat that had done ten years' service ; pulled on his thin, pointed, elastic-sided boots, and shuffled out into the sun carrying his parcel under his arm. He was not free from Hell until he was free of it. But it would fetch twenty pounds !

As the old man shuffled down the street eyes watched him from window after window. He was to the broken poor of Ormeston what certain financial houses are to The Masters of Europe. They feared, they hated, they obeyed ; and while he shuffled on few men whom he met would fail, if he met them alone, to do his bidding.

Mr. Montague's God sent him a man standing alone, or rather lounging alone, a man reclining against the corner wall of a house called, I regret to say, "The Pork Pie," and already doomed in the eyes of the unflinching magistrates of Ormeston : doomed at a price to one of their own members who was the proprietor thereof : a price to be paid in public gold.

The transaction between the · receiver and the lounger was not long in doing. Mr. Montague approached the lounger with that unmistakable air of a master, which you will also note when, in another world, a financier approaches a politician. With that unmistakable air of the servant which, in another world, you will note when the politician receives the financier, did the lounger receive Mr. Montague.

The lounger did not stiffen or straighten himself to express his inferiority to the old man. There was nothing military in their relations. But he contrived as he lounged to look more abject, more crapulous than ever. And as the aged receiver with a few hoarse words in his low tones handed the parcel over, the lounger took it. He was pleased to hear Mr. Montague's command, though it had been given with a filthy oath, that he might sell where he would the contents of that paper, but Mr. Montague (who knew what happened to every man) demanded half the proceeds, and so left him. When these words had passed the old man shuffled off, and the

lounger thought of him no more, save as a dread
master, whom he would certainly serve, to whom he
would most certainly pay his due, and also as a
benefactor in a way.

But when he had rid himself of the violent and
dreadful thing, and given his order and claimed his
due, what Mr. Montague did was this. He boarded
a tram in a neighbouring parallel street. He paid
his halfpenny, and went right to the Lydgate, an
old quarter of the town, now full of slums, wherein
dwelt a certain Pole of the name of Lipsky.

He had taken the most rapid means he could,
but even so he glanced nervously over his shoulder
lest a lounger with a parcel should be following.

What Lipsky, a Pole, with his distant strange name,
might mean to a man bearing that old crusading,
western name of Montague no one has ever known.

Some say he was a son, which was surely impossible ; some a cousin, which is unlikely ; for
do the Montagues wed the Lipskys ?

The tram passed by the door of that little clothes
shop—a whole front of slops with huge white ticket-
prices on them—and above the word " Lipsky " in
large letters of gold on brown. Mr. Montague
shuffled off the tram and shuffled to the door of
that place of business.

He found Mr. Lipsky alone at the counter within.

Mr. Montague had not a moment to spare, and
in that moment he had passed the word about the
Green Overcoat.

Mr. Lipsky was incredulous. There was no one

else in the little slop-shop. The elder man leant over the counter and whispered in his ear. And the word that he whispered was not an English word. The younger man took on a different colour. It was like cheese changing to chalk.

" Vah ! " said the Pole. " Not keep it ? Vy not ? Keep it, sell it—that 's business ! Keep it as long as should be and sell it at best price. Not keep it ? Thems superstition ! "

Mr. Montague said no more. He had done his duty. Whatever the Pole might suffer—if—by chance—that Green Overcoat should come his way, *his* conscience was clear. The office which Crusaders owe to Poles was fulfilled. He had not despoiled his brethren.

He was off, was Mr. Montague, shuffling out of the little shop hurriedly across the tramway line of the Lydgate, and back by devious and narrow ways to his mean house. An odd relief filled him as he walked, and an odd lightness as he entered. He had got rid of an accursed thing. And it so happened that when he reached that filthy little room of his, as sleep was overpowering him, he knelt and prayed to a God of the Hills, a strange and vengeful but triumphant God, who had saved his servant Montague.

CHAPTER XI

In which a Pole is less scrupulous

THE name of the lounger was James. That was his Christian name. What his family name might be it is impossible to discover at this distance of time, for he had been born in 1868, brought up in the workhouse, apprenticed to a ropemaker, passed various terms in jail under various *aliases*, gone to sea, naturalised as an American citizen, returned to England as valet in the service of a tourist, been dismissed a few years before for theft, and was at this moment a member of the New Bureaucracy, to wit, a Watcher and Checker under the Ormeston Labour Exchange. He was paid (by results, 2*s*. 6*d*. for each conviction) to see that the poor did not cheat the higher officials of that invaluable Public office, to worm out the true history of applicants at the Exchange, and to provide secret evidence against them, that they might be imprisoned and black-listed if they concealed their past from the Secretary —a Valued Servant of the State.

James, then, wandered out into God's great world upon that happy morning with a bundle under his arm. Two conflicting thoughts disturbed him. First, where he might sell the content at the highest

price, and, secondly, where he might sell it with the
greatest security.   Such divergent issues disturb the
great men of our time as well as wandering men
bearing alien coats ; they are at the root of modern
affairs.

The moré he thought of it the more did James
determine by the feel that the bundle was *clothes ;*
why, then, his market was a shop in the Lydgate,
an old quarter of the town, now full of slums, wherein
dwelt a certain Pole of the name of Lipsky.   This
man, by common repute, was well with the police,
and in our English towns that, with the poor, is
everything.   Lippy would not give him full value,
but he could give him full security.   He would
give him perhaps but a quarter of the value, but he
would at least give him a free run with the money
and no awkward questions for the men in blue.

Such an advantage is it to have assured the police
of one's integrity.

Nevertheless, he thought it of advantage to
discover of what value the bundle might be.   Even
if he was to get but a quarter of its value from the
Pole, he would like to know *what* it was that he was
to get a quarter of.

He lollopped lazily down the street.   His time
was his own.   He peered through a neglected doorway into an empty yard, stepped into it, behind the
screen of a hoarding, looking first up and down to
see whether any of the tyrants were about.   Seeing
no helmet and therefore no tyrant, he untied the
parcel and pulled out the coat within.   He was

agreeably surprised. He had expected slops, but
this was not slops. He was no valuer, but he would
imperil for ever the true end of man's soul and suffer
the companionship of demons for eternity (such were
the rash hazards he took) if it were not two quid, and
played properly it might be three.

Wait a moment, there might be something in the
pockets. He felt in the left-hand pocket—nothing ;
in the right-hand pocket, there nothing but that
solid, oblong cheque book with four cheques torn out.
At first he thought of throwing it away, for it
identified the owner of the garment. Then he
remembered things called "clues," and threw far
from him the very idea instead of the cheque book.
He tried to decipher the name, but could not. James
could read and write when he had left school, but
that was a long time ago. He had done more useful
work since then.

Next he remembered the suspicious haste of
Mr. Montague. He began to wonder whether the
bundle was quite *safe*. He determined to hurry ;
and as for the price, why, he would take what he
could get.

He fastened up the parcel again, and in a sobriety
of mind which was new to him and not altogether
pleasant, he took the road to the Lydgate. Mr.
Montague might have spared his fears. The day
was early, James had as yet no pence, he could not
board a tram. But somehow or other the bundle
was unnaturally clumsy or unnaturally heavy.

He felt a distaste for it. The distaste enlarged,

something had gone wrong. As he went down that
morning street alone, resolutely trudging, he heard
within him the echoes of a voice he did not wish to
hear. It was the voice of a woman, not sober, but
holding to him. He thought he could not have
remembered such a thing after ten years, and of a
summer morning. It is odd that even the poor
should mislike such memories ; James misliked them
abominably. Perhaps he was more sensitive for
the moment than are most of the poor. . . .

Yes ! How she did drink, damn her. . . . Why
the Hell was he thinking of such things ? And how
clear her voice was. . . . Then he saw the name
" Lipsky " over the way. He was at the Lydgate
already. Could a man be drunk in the flush of
morning and without liquor ? Nay, drink dulled
such things, and he had heard that voice awfully
clear within him.

He trudged into the shop, shaking his mind free,
and thinking of the sovereign—or two sovereigns
at least.

The gentleman in charge—there was but one—
exchanged mutual recognitions with James. The
one was a Pole and the other an Englishman ; but
both were human, and therefore brethren. Then
James untied the parcel. But when James had
untied the parcel it was apparent that though both
were human, Lipsky was a Pole and not a man of
the Midlands, for he thrust it from him with his palms
outward, sliding his wrists upon the counter, and
moving his fingers like small snakes in the air.

Lippy was not taking any. James looked at him, and did not understand.

"I got it straight, I did!" he said.

Lippy didn't want to look at it.

"I don't want it, there!" burst out James (he could not for his life have told you why), and Lippy, leaning over familiarly but insolently, told him (in Polish English) that if he tried to sell it he would not long be a free man. James thought this treason, and in his heart he was determined on revenge. What had he done to Lippy to receive such a threat? The whole air about these men as they met, and as this lump of cloth lay between them, was unreal and fantastic. Each felt it, each in his utterly different mind. For such things, if you will excuse me, happen to the poor also, as we all know they do to the rich, whether through drink or what-not I can't tell, whether for drink or what-not it is for them to determine. There was fate, and there was compulsion, and there was the profound ill-ease of the soul hovering over that dirty counter in the slums as they hover over the tables of politicians when similar bargains are toward in a larger world. James tied his bundle up again and went out without a word.

One beefy part of him suggested that the coppers were too close on the trail and that Lippy knew it; but another part of him, more permanent, more real, deeper, smelt the truth. He himself had suffered dread; he felt vaguely that Lippy knew the cause of that dread, and that for both of them

there was something strange about the Thing. The
Soul was in trouble.

Oh ! James knew it very well. The big bundle
under his left arm so weighed upon that primal part
of us, which is within, that all the things least desired
and most carefully forgotten of his life returned
again under its influence and maddened him. With
the simplicity of his class, he thought the evil to be
attached to the fact that the coat was stolen. Unlike
his betters, he had never dreamt that stealing was
right. He had always known that it was wrong.
. . . He had a mind to put the Green Overcoat
down in the thoroughfare and leave it there. In spite
of the risk, he would have done so in another moment
had he not heard shuffling footsteps coming up rapidly
behind him and felt a soft Polish hand upon his
shoulder. It was Lippy.

The Poles when they enter the Second Hand
Clothes Trade prove themselves commercial. Their
ancient chivalry seems to desert them in this line
of business, and something material creeps into their
gallant hearts. Lippy had reproached himself,
Lippy had been tortured as he had seen the lounger's
figure slowly and doubtfully receding burdened with
a thing of so much value.

With the disappearance of the Green Overcoat
the supernatural warnings (for which he despised
himself) had disappeared, and he remembered only
its very mundane value. He could not bear the loss,
and he had followed.

The lounger James turned round startled, and

instinctively thrust the bundle towards the man who, he instinctively knew, had repented of his first decision. Lippy seized it, guiltily, furtively, violently, and without a word he was on his way back to his shop. But as for James, he went his way noting suddenly the pleasantness of the morning ; that excellent Watcher and Checker under the Labour Exchange of Ormeston, that Pillar of Free Labour, that Good Servant of the State, that member of our New Bureaucracy of Social Reform, was himself again. He went forward whistling, and he found it in a few moments quite easy to forget the Thing and all the memories that had cropped up with the Thing. He had passed it on, and Lippy was holding the baby.

In the few steps to his shop the Pole had no time to repent, though his mind was ill at ease. Mr. Montague was a strange man. He had strange wisdom. He could read strange books. And if Mr. Montague had come to warn him, well . . .

Lippy dismissed the superstitious fear. He opened the bundle, he gazed on the Sacred Green Thing, he felt the pockets (of course), he saw the cheque book and the wealthy name. He shuddered—but he gloried. Then he fastened the whole up again, put the bundle into a great drawer under his counter, sighed a mechanical sigh of mechanical relief, and began to busy himself with the arranging and ticketing of his goods for the day.

But as that day wore on the Pole was not himself. He was too nervous, too snappy with customers,

too much affected by slight sounds when the evening
came, and all that night he lay but dozing, waking
continually in starts from disordered dreams of
unaccountable vengeance.

The next day, the Friday, Lippy was very ill.
No movement of conscience disturbed him, he had
not wronged his own ; yet in his fever he suffered
dreadfully from some unreasoning sense of evil.•

The old woman who chared for him was for calling
a doctor.   All Monday Lippy, weakening in his sick-
bed, fought against the expense.   As it was, he had
been compelled to pay a doubtful boy—a non-Pole,
and therefore ill suited to commerce—to mind the
shop, and twice he left his bed, at the risk of his
life, and tottered down to see that no harm was
coming to his business.   On each occasion as he
neared that counter with its drawer and its secreted
bundle a more violent trouble had returned, and he
had had to be helped up dazed and trembling to
his wretched bed and room above.

So Monday passed, and what happened on the
Tuesday and why, a return to others who had
meddled with the Green Overcoat will explain :
Why on the morning of Tuesday Lippy woke
refreshed in body, but very weak ; why he had an
odd feeling that things were mending, how he could
not tell ; why it was that in the early afternoon of
that day he heard in the shop below a voice addressing
his assistant in an accent very unusual to such shops ;
why Lippy listened carefully at the door and thought
he knew the voice.

The voice you will find, Readerkin, was that of
Mr. Kirby, and Mr. Kirby was asking in the most
direct fashion possible for the coat, for the Green
Overcoat ; he made no bones about it, he put it
square. Very hurriedly did Lippy dress, and very
hurriedly, weak as he was, did he totter down the
stairs that Tuesday Morning.

CHAPTER XII

In which the Readerkin will, if he has an ounce of Brains, begin to catch the inevitable Denoumong of the Imbroglio

MONDAY is the first working day of the week : and upon Monday—at least on *some* Mondays—Mr. Kirby actually went to his office.

Mr. Kirby so far loved duty or routine or respected the tradition of centuries—or anything else you like—as to visit his office upon *some* Mondays at sometime or other in the forenoon. It was a superstition with which he could not break, sensible as he would have been to have broken with it. His ample and increasing income proceeded mainly from investment ; he was utterly devoid of avarice ; he had neither family nor heirs. He was delighted that his junior partners should do the work, and they were welcome to the financial result of it. But still, the firm was Kirby and Blake, and his name *was* Kirby, and I think he had an inward feeling, unexpressed, that he stood a little better with his fellow-citizens of Ormeston, and with his very numerous friends, if he kept up the appearance of visiting the place—on some Mondays.

Anyhow, visit it he did—usually as long after eleven as he dared ; and leave it he did—usually as

long before one as his conscience would let him.
Invariably did he say that he would return in the
afternoon, and almost invariably did he fail to do
so, save perhaps to look in vacantly, ask a few
irrelevant questions, glance at his watch, say that he
was late for some appointment—and go out again.

There were, indeed, occasions when the familiar
advice upon which the chief of his acquaintances
depended necessitated a formal interview at the
office : commonly he preferred to conduct such
things in their private houses or his own. Fortune
favoured him in this much, that the very short time
he spent at his place of business was not usually
productive of anxiety or even of a client whom he
personally must see. But upon this Monday, as it
so happened, his luck failed him.

It was a quarter to twelve when he came briskly
in wearing that good-humoured and rather secret
smile, nodded to the clerks, passed into his own
room, and proceeded to do his duty as a solicitor by
reaching for the telephone, with the object of
reserving a table for lunch at the club. As he was
in the midst of this professional occupation, a clerk,
to his intense annoyance, begged him to receive as a
matter of urgency a Mr. Postlethwaite. The name
was familiar to Mr. Kirby, and he groaned in spirit.

" Oh, Mr. Blake can see him ! " he said impatiently.
" No, he can't ; no, I remember, he can't."

He scratched his chin and managed to frown at
the forehead without relaxing that small perpetual
smile.

"Send him in here," he sighed ; " and look here, Thurston, has he got anything with him ? "

" Not that I could see, sir," answered the clerk respectfully.

" Oh, I don't mean a dog or a sister-in-law," replied Mr. Kirby without dignity and somewhat impatiently. " I mean a damned great roll of paper."

" Well, sir," said Thurston the clerk with continued respect, " he certainly carried something of that sort in his hand."

" Show him in, Thurston, show him in," said Mr. Kirby louder than ever, and leaning back in his chair. . . .

He knew this old Postlethwaite of old, a man of grievances, a man whom it was the lawyer's business to dissuade from law ; a man whom he couldn't quite call mad, but a man whom Mr. Kirby certainly did not trust with any member of the firm ; a man with whose considerable business in scattered freeholds (quite twenty of them up and down the suburbs of Ormeston, and nearly all of the munfortunate investments) Kirby in a moment of generosity or folly—perhaps rather of freakishness—had undertaken for his firm to let and sell and value, and now he wished he hadn't !

For as Mr. Postlethwaite grew older, he grew more frightening, and he was a man now nearly seventy years of age. But his years had in no way diminished his almost epileptic vigour. Mr. Kirby could hear the terrible tramp of his great boots and the exclamations of his great voice in the corridor. The door opened, and he came in. He stood tall and menacing in the entry, and slammed the door behind him. His abundant white hair tumbled in great shocks over his head, his ill-kept beard bristled upon all sides from his face, and his eyes, which were reddish in colour (horrible thought!), glared like coals. His greeting was not friendly, but it was at least direct.

"You got me into this, Kirby," he shouted by way of good morning, "and you 've got to get me out!"

If Mr. Kirby disliked business, he certainly loved an adventure. His permanent smile grew more lively. His sinewy neck seemed to shorten, he thrust his determined chin a trifle forward, and said with a wave of his hand—

"Pray sit down, Mr. Postlethwaite, I am entirely at your service."

"I 'll not sit down," roared the redoubtable Postlethwaite. "You got me into this, and you 've got to get me out!"

"And of which," said Mr. Kirby, in a tone of intelligent politeness, "of which of your tomfooleries may you be speaking?"

Mr. Postlethwaite, like most of his kind, was rather relieved by insults than fired by them.

"I 'll show you," he said fiercely, but in a more business-like tone than before. "You 'll see! . . . And when you 've seen, I 'll thank you to think twice before you get me in a worse hole than ever," and as he said these words he spread out upon Mr. Kirby's table a fairly large sheet of cartridge paper, neat, but bearing marks of age, and having drawn upon it in the various colours of the architect the elevation and plans of a house standing in small grounds. There was marked a lodge, a ground floor, a first floor and a second ; at the back a small enclosed backyard, and in the side elevation could be seen let into the high steep roof of the topmost story a large skylight. It was beautifully tinted in blue.

"Architects do imitate nature well !" said Mr. Kirby half to himself. "It 's Greystones !" and he chuckled.

"You needn't laugh, Kirby !" thundered the aged Postlethwaite. "Oh, you 'll laugh the other side of your mouth before I 've done ! Ruined, Kirby ! Smashed ! Destroyed ! And no clue !"

Mr. Kirby put up his hand.

"Please, Mr. Postlethwaite, please," he said. "If the place is burnt down I congratulate you."

"'Tisn't !" snapped Postlethwaite.

"Well, if it 's partially burnt down all the better. They 're more ready to pay when . . ."

"Not burnt at all !" snarled Mr. Postlethwaite loudly. "Broken ! Destroyed ! Smashed ! Went there this morning ! Didn't find anybody !"

"They 'd gone out ?" said Mr. Kirby, with a look of aquiline cunning.

"No one anywhere ! Nothing anywhere ! No one on the ground floor ! No one first floor ! No one *top floor !* No one in the studio ! But there ! Smashed ! Broken ! Destroyed !"

"What was?" said Mr. Kirby, beginning to be irritated as he thought of the possible delay to his lunch.

"What?" shouted Mr. Postlethwaite, "everything I tell you! Skylight, chairs, everything. Broken chair in the garden with a lot of sheets tied on. Damned foolery! Broken chairs, broken glass, empty bottle, beastly dirty mess of food. Now," he added, with rising passion, "I'll have the law on this, and it's you who did it, Kirby, it's you persuaded me!"

"Mr. Postlethwaite," said Mr. Kirby quietly, "what I did try to persuade you was to spend a little money on the place. As you wouldn't, and as a tramp wouldn't look at it, I advised you to let it to those young fellows for a month. I knew all about them, at least one of them, the one who came to me—James McAuley. He's perfectly all right. Said he wanted to paint with his friend. I know his father, big doctor in London. Boy was at Cambridge. They're as right as rain, Postlethwaite. If they've hurt your property we can get compensation. The month's not up by a long while, and hang it, I did get you prepayment!"

"*We* can't get compensation?" huffed Mr. Postlethwaite. "*I* shall!"

"Yes, *you* will, of course," corrected Mr. Kirby quietly. "Do make some sort of connected story for me. When did you go to Greystones?"

"Just come from it," said the aged Postlethwaite glaringly. "All smashed! Broken! Destroyed!"

"Did you find any letter, or note, or anything?"

"Nothing. Told you. Quite empty. And a dirty piece of rope chucked up into the rafters as well," he added, as though that were the worst and last -of his grievances. "Where are those young scoundrels ? "

"My dear Mr. Postlethwaite," said the lawyer suavely, "it isn't actionable here between four walls. But if you say that kind of thing outside you might find yourself in Queer Street. Those excellent young men—that excellent young James McAuley—paid you for the month in advance. You 've no proof they did the damage."

"They 're responsible," said Mr. Postlethwaite doggedly, "so are you. Last man six months ago was a vegetarian. Tried to raise spirits in the place. *Did* raise them. Haunted now, for all I know. All your fault."

"Now, Mr. Postlethwaite," said Mr. Kirby firmly, "one thing at a time. If you have let Greystones get into that condition against my advice, you have been exceedingly lucky to get two tenants, mad or sane, for even a few weeks in the course of a year. Upon my soul, I 'm getting tired of Greystones, and all the rest of 'em. I 've a good mind . . ."

As a matter of fact, Mr. Kirby had no good mind to give up his connection with Greystones or with any other of old Mr. Postlethwaite's follies. They were almost the only thing in his profession which amused him.

"Well, what are you going to do ? " snapped the old gentleman again.

"Go round and see it, I think," said Mr. Kirby, "and you come with me."

Mr. Postlethwaite was somewhat mollified. His lawyer was taking a little trouble. It was as it should be.

They took a taxi and found themselves, twenty minutes or so, outside the town, passing the deserted lodge and the scarecrow, mouldy gate, and drawing up 'before the stone steps of that deserted, unfurnished, ramshackle house which had been Professor Higginson's purgatory for three long days. The two men went in together, and Mr. Kirby noted that old Postlethwaite had been accurate enough. There were the dirty windows, the uncarpeted staircase, the bench and table in the right-hand ground-floor room which were the sole furniture of the lower part of the house ; and there, when they came upstairs to it, was the wreckage in the studio—the broken skylight, the scraps of food, the wooden chairs lying smashed on the floor.

"Where did you find the third chair ? Funny sort of house. Silly of you not to mend it !" he said, with a return to his habit of irrelevance.

"Told you !" said Mr. Postlethwaite. "Outside on the ground. Lot of sheets tied to it like the tail of a kite."

"Box kites have no tails," murmured Mr. Kirby, "he must have thrown it."

"Who ? " asked Mr. Postlethwaite eagerly.

"*I* don't know," said Mr. Kirby with charming innocence.

"You're making a fool of me!" said old Mr. Postlethwaite savagely.

"No, I'm not," returned Mr. Kirby in a soothing tone. "Come, there's nothing more to be done here. I'll write to those young men. I'll write at once. I'll hear the day after to-morrow, and I'll let you know."

"The day after to-morrow!" shrieked old Mr. Postlethwaite. "And the house wide open, and anyone coming in through that skylight?"

"It'd be a charity," said the lawyer. "It will shelter the little birds."

Mr. Kirby made to put his arm into the angry old gentleman's and to lead him down the stairs, when he noticed something on the floor. It was a scrap of paper. He picked it up, glanced at it hurriedly, and put it in his pocket. Then—the gesture had taken but a moment—he was holding Mr. Postlethwaite's arm and taking him down the stairs.

"You ought to have a caretaker here for a day or two anyhow, Postlethwaite," said Mr. Kirby as they reached the door. "I know a man in a cottage here, I'll send him."

Mr. Postlethwaite was agreeable. Mr. Kirby called at the cottage and sent the man up. Then he came back to the cab.

"I'll try and get to hear from McAuley to-day," went on the lawyer, as they got into the taxi again and returned to Ormeston. "By the way, what would you take for Greystones, Postlethwaite?"

He knew what was coming. Mr. Postlethwaite's face grew dark and determined. Then there passed over it a not very sane leer. He nudged the lawyer in the ribs—

"Twenty-five thousand," he said, "not a penny less."

"Make it pence," said Mr. Kirby, with more than usual gravity.

Old Mr. Postlethwaite disdained to reply.

"Town's growing out that side," he said in a tone of immense cunning. "Not a penny less."

"Well," said Mr. Kirby in a weary tone, "if you won't set fire to it, I don't know how you're going to realise, and upon my soul I don't care."

The taxi had drawn up at the door of Mr. Kirby's club. He resolutely refused to pursue matters further with the aged speculator in freehold values.

"Postlethwaite," he said, "you may take it from me if you are wise. *Wait . . .*"

Then he added most unprofessionally—

"If I got thirty thousand would you give me half the difference as commission?"

Old Postlethwaite looked up suddenly and brightly like a bird.

"What! Five thousand?" he said doubtfully.

He shook his head. He knew that it was not very professional. He looked to see that no one was coming out of the club, and then he whispered—

"Three thousand, Kirby, three thousand! And that's ten per cent.," he added half regretfully.

"'All right," said Mr. Kirby with due solemnity, "you wait!'" and with a reassuring smile he dismissed that poor old man to dream of impossible sums.

Whether Mr. Kirby thought that the house could have fetched five hundred pounds—or nothing at all—does not really matter to my story, for most undoubtedly he had no hope or intention of selling the wretched place at all unless some lunatic should clamour for it.

He went into the club as into a city of refuge, and prepared to consider a number of little disconnected events that were shaping themselves into a very pretty scheme. Things were beginning to entertain him vastly. It was the sort of work he liked.

First he countermanded his lunch. He wanted to think, not eat. Next he pulled from his pocket the little slip of paper he had picked up at Greystones. He read it carefully. It told him little, but that little was curious.

The paper was University paper. It had the University Arms. It seemed to be jotted notes.

He laid it down a moment, and considered one or two other unaccountable, disconnected matters. Brassington's Coat, Brassington's Secret God, the Green Coat. Brassington's fetish—gone. Gone quite unexplained, and gone—let 's see—just a week ago. Missed that Monday night at Perkin's. A young gentleman, " a friend of the young master's," who had called at " Lauderdale " that day and had asked too many questions about Mr. Brassington's movements. Mr. Kirby smiled broadly, and remembered suddenly the letting of Greystones some days before. How old Jock McAuley's son— Jimmy, the name was—had come with pompousness

of youth and bargained to have Greystones for a
month. " To paint," he said. " To paint with a
friend ! " Yes ˊ. . . To paint things red ! Mr.
Kirby smiled broadly again. He saw nothing
clear. He saw an imbroglio forming, and he gloried
in such things !

It looked as though that young man and his
friend had painted thoroughly ! . . . They had
had a lark . . . and what a lark ! Well, they
must pay the piper ! . . . They had made a night
of it. . . . With whom ?

Mr. Kirby lay back in his very comfortable chair
in the smoking-room of the club and pondered.
. . . Someone who went to the lectures at the
Guelph University here in Ormeston had been in
that rough and tumble in Greystones. . . . It
had been a students' rag he supposed.

He took up the crumpled slip of paper once more
and opened it out again carefully. As he tried to
connect the disjointed phrases scribbled upon it he
got a bit puzzled.

What student would want such notes as these ?

" Memorandum : Horne does not agree with
Latouche. Mention this to-morrow in the first
hour. Return both essays.

" The second year work in future to be combined
with the Medical. Announce this at end of first
hour."

Mr. Kirby pursed his lips and considered those
words. It was a Professor's memorandum . . .

and it was not the sort of notes that a Professor would hand to a pupil either.

There was something else jotted in the same hand, but written smaller, in the corner. He peered at it and made it out at last, though it was hurriedly written as though it were a sort of after-thought :—

"Ask the Senate next Monday to cancel Saturday afternoon, difficult hour. Remember Garden's number, to ring up 637 Ormeston Central."

Mr. Kirby folded the paper in its original creases, put it back into his pocket-book, and stretched for the University *Calendar*, which was among the reference books on a table beside him.

There was more than one of these Saturday afternoon lectures. The Senate had arranged them for popular courses, and the University men rather resented them. There was one with History for its subject, one whole set called " Roman Art of the First Century" (and Mr. Kirby grinned), one course on the Geological Formation of Oil Areas, one course on Psychology, and one on French Literature.

History, Art, Geology, Psychology, French.

Methodically, but with all the pleasure of the chase, Mr. Kirby turned to the Professors in occupancy of the five various chairs. Polson, Gaunt, Baker, Higginson, Rolls.

Then he bethought him which of these comic things the enfranchised and cultured proletariat could bear least. He decided very rightly that it lay between Roman Art and Psychology. Gaunt was the Art man, a charlatan. He knew him. He remembered doing his best to prevent the appointment. The Psychology man, Higginson, he had met here and there, as everyone met the University people in Ormeston, but he could call up no very clear picture of him : his was a recent appointment, and the town did not yet know the new Professor well.

If it were either of those two men who had been larking with younger men that night when old Postlethwaite's house was turned upside down, why, he thought it would probably be Gaunt.

The problem which was beginning to fascinate and enthrall Mr. Kirby would have advanced a stage or two further towards its solution had not the swing door of the smoking-room been flung up, and had there not burst through it, like a shell, the excited and angry form of Mr. Brassington.

Mr. Kirby hated business : he hated worry. His delight was to think things out. And therefore it was that Providence, which chastens those whom it loves, disturbed him with this sudden and most unquiet apparition of his close friend. Mr. Brassington's usually careful clothes were crumpled, his face was all a-sweat, his tie was quite dreadfully on one side, almost under his ear.

The merchant staggered up to the lawyer, put one hand on his shoulder, and said hoarsely—

" Forgery ! "

Mr. Kirby firmly pushed his friend down into a chair.

"Forgery?" he asked in an interested tone, looking Mr. Brassington straight in the face.

Mr. Brassington nodded.

"Well, my dear Brassington," continued Mr. Kirby, "I will do what I can for you, but I warn you it is a very difficult crime to defend a man for."

"What do you mean?" said Mr. Brassington, bewildered.

"Besides which," went on Mr. Kirby in a judicial tone, "unless you plead lunacy —— "

"I don't understand a word you're saying, Kirby," shouted Mr. Brassington. "There's been forgery! Do you hear? Forgery! Someone's been forging my name!"

"O—o—oh!" said Mr. Kirby in a reasonable tone. "Someone's been forging *your* name? Much more sensible! Bring it off?" he added cheerfully.

"If I didn't know you so well, Kirby . . ." began Mr. Brassington savagely, then dragging from an inner pocket an already dirty cheque, and presenting it with a trembling hand, he said—

"There, look at that!"

Mr. Kirby looked at it in front, then he looked at it behind. He saw that a Mr. James McAuley had touched two thousand. He looked at the front again. He turned it round and looked at the endorsement. He looked closely at the signature.

"No," he said, putting the slip of paper close to his eyes, "that's not your signature, as you say, but" (musing thoughtfully) "it's very, very like it!"

"Kirby," said Mr. Brassington, in tones quite new

and dreadfully solemn, " I 've a son myself . . .
but that young man shall suffer the full weight of
the law ! "

Mr. Kirby was looking out of the window.

" What young man ? " he said innocently.

" James McAuley," said Mr. Brassington in a
slow, deep tone, making the most of the long vowel.

" How do you know he 's a young man ? " said
Mr. Kirby, looking round with interest.

" How do I know ? " shouted Mr. Brassington,
beginning to storm again. " Why, that 's the
impudent scoundrel that robbed my poor son, sir !
Robbed him at cards ! And I tell you what, Kirby,"
he added, his voice rising more and more angrily,
" I tell you what, he 's calculating on it, that 's what
he 's doing. He 's counting on my wanting to hush
it up. My wanting to hush up my poor son's fatal
weakness."

" Fatal what ? " said Mr. Kirby.

" Weakness," said Mr. Brassington, suddenly pulled
up.

" Oh ! " said Mr. Kirby quite coolly. " So he 's
the chap that forged the cheque, is he ? "

" Of course ! " said the indignant Mr. Brassington.

" Well," replied Mr. Kirby, " I hope you 've got
proof, that 's all ! And I hope, if you *haven't* got
proof, that you haven't been talking to anybody else !
For if you can't prove that he did it it 's *slander*,
you know. You 're a rich man, Brassington !
You 're the kind of man these gentry like to go for,
eh ? "

Mr. Brassington, like most of his fellow-subjects, lay in a panic terror of lawyers and their arts. He was appreciably paler when he answered in a far more subdued tone.

" I don't exactly say he did it, I wouldn't say more than I can prove, would I ? Only," and here his voice rose again, " he's got the money out of me somehow, and . . ."

" Now look here, Brassington," said Mr. Kirby quietly, " will you leave this-with me ? "

As Mr. Kirby said this he put his head somewhat on one side, thrust his hands into his pockets, and got the seated Mr. Brassington into focus.

" No—er—yes—if you like," said Mr. Brassington. " How long ? "

Mr. Kirby put his hand before his face and leant his elbow upon the mantelpiece.

" I don't know," he said after a few moments. " It may be three or four days, or it may be more, or it may be less. Look here," he added, " will you let me send for you if I get a clue ? I think I shall get one . . . What a huge balance you must keep."

" If that young scoundrel ——" began Mr. Brassington again.

" Now, my dear Brassington," said Mr. Kirby soothingly, " my dear Brassington, the man may be as innocent as, well ——"

" You don't suspect my son, I suppose ? " broke in Mr. Brassington fiercely.

Mr. Kirby laughed pleasantly.

" Good Lord, no ! " he said. " Don't you see,

Brassington, life 's a complicated place. Supposing
a man knew that your son owed McAuley this ——"

"Owed it !" thundered Mr. Brassington. "And how
in the name of justice can this accursed gambling——"

"Now ! Now ! Now !" said Mr. Kirby. "We
won't go into that !   The point is, that supposing
someone *did* know that this chap McAuley, at any
rate, thought it was owed him ? "

"He   couldn't   have   thought   so," said   Mr.
Brassington stubbornly.

"Oh, Nonsense !" said Mr. Kirby, almost at the
end of his patience. "Supposing someone knew that
McAuley would take the money, there ——"

"Well ? " said Mr. Brassington.

"Well, then, don't you see, he might make himself
out a go-between and take a commission ? "

"If I get the man ——" began Mr. Brassington
again.

"Yes, yes, I know," said Mr. Kirby, "but you 've
left that to me, and it 's very wise of you. . . .
There 's another thing you ought to have left to me.
I 'm good at that sort of thing. And that 's your
Green Overcoat."

Mr. Brassington started.

"Oh, I know you 're superstitious, Brassington.
All you hard-headed, business men, or whatever you
call yourselves, those that have got any brains at least
(and there aren't many) show their brains by a little
superstition. That 's my experience. I don't blame
you. Only look here. If I get it for you . . ."
and he began musing.

"I'm not superstitious, Kirby," said Mr. Brassington uncomfortably.

He rose as though the very mention of the garment had disturbed him.

"It's just a coincidence. Things do go wrong," he added.

When he had said this he moved to go.

"I'm sorry," said Kirby, "I didn't know you felt so strongly about it. Or rather I did know, and I oughtn't to have spoken."

Mr. Brassington was still confused. He did not answer, and he made to go out.

Mr. Kirby did not detain him, but just as his friend was opening the door he said—

"Brassington, can you show me the counterfoil to that cheque?"

"No, I can't," said Brassington. "Book's gone. It was in the Overcoat."

"Oh, the book's gone too!" said Mr. Kirby. "Well, I hope you've stopped all the remaining numbers in the Cheque Book?"

"Yes," said Mr. Brassington doggedly.

Mr. Kirby thought a moment.

"Brassington," he said, "I've got to be in London on Wednesday. And I'm going to the Rockingham. I'm going to give a dinner. Will you come? Will you come early—and, I say—bring your son—bring Algernon. Come by five o'clock. I'll be waiting."

"I'll come," said Mr. Brassington—as though asking why.

" I may have news for you," said Mr. Kirby.

Brassington looked at him doubtfully, and he was gone.

Hardly was his friend out of the room when Mr. Kirby, with something of the gesture that a dog with a good nose will make when he is getting interested, made for the writing table, and noted the appointment.

" Before I forget it," he murmured. " Wednesday, the Rockingham, five—and dinner 's seven. I wish I hadn't had to make a day in such a hurry—but it 'll serve . . . I can always change it," he thought.

Then he visualised young McAuley quite carefully and clearly. He did these sort of things better when his eyes were fixed upon a glare. He gazed, therefore, hard at a sunlit white wall in a court opposite the club window, and as he did so he saw McAuley again quite clearly. The fresh, vigorous, young Celtic face with its dark and sincere eyes. . . . And he wondered who on earth could have taken that young man in ! Then he sighed a little, and said to himself, aloud—

" But it 's easy to believe anything for two thousand pounds ! "

Mr. Kirby left the smoking-room. On his way out through the hall he did something that would have astonished those many million innocents who swallow our daily press.

He went to the telephone and rang up 246. 246 answered very gruffly ; then, suddenly appreciating that it was Mr. Kirby who was talking, 246 answered with extraordinary courtesy.

Since I may only report what happened at my end of the line, let the reader gather what it was that Mr. Kirby said.

He said—

" Is that you, Robinson ? "

Next he said—

" Any other inspector there ? "

The third thing he said was—

" No ! No ! Mr. Brassington's coat ! Advertised, you fool ! "

The fourth thing he said was—

" It isn't a question of whether the receiver admitted it, but what receiver you traced it to."

The fifth thing was said very impatiently—

" Oh, yes, yes, of course, I know Mr. Brassington must have asked. The point is, *which* . . . What ? . . . Spell it ! M—O—N—T . . . Oh, yes . . . Old Sammy ! " Then came a pause. " *What ?* . . . Didn't go any further ? . . . Done nothing more all these days ? . . . Good Heavens . . ." A shorter pause. Then, " All right . . . Oh, never mind about what you *didn't* find ! " and he rang off.

Thus did Mr. Kirby discover all he wanted to know.

Strange ! But there are quite unofficial people, not even dressed up in blue clothes and a helmet, who are in touch with such things as receivers of stolen goods, and the financiers of the poor and the local Trust in Crime. Men who can promote or dismiss the mighty Perlice Themselves !—and these beings are often Lawyers.

Now that he was fairly in cry, he did what no dog does—not even the dogs that boast they are hounds —he slacked off. He lunched well. He smoked half through the afternoon. With the evening he lounged off to his office before it should close to see if anything new awaited him there : and something did.

CHAPTER XIII

In which the Subliminal Consciousness gives itself away

THE work of the Sunday had tired . Professor Higginson. He did not know that glory could weary man so much.

He rose very late upon the Monday morning : he rose certainly without ambition, and almost without fear. He was dead beat. By the time he had breakfasted it was noon. He had no class on Monday. In the early afternoon he was due at the Council of the University. He remembered the agenda, more or less. He had to talk particularly about those Saturday lectures. He hated them— but first of all he must ring up his colleague Garden, who was with him in the matter.

Garden had the telephone—sensible man ! But Garden wouldn't allow his number in the book . . . It was ? . . . It was 37 something ? . . . Wait a minute ! Professor Higginson

7

remembered a scrap of paper with a memorandum. *That* had the number. He had put it down *last* Monday on a scrap of paper after the Senate meeting for just that occasion, to ring up Garden before the Council.

He had a good memory. He prided himself on *that*. He clearly remembered jotting the number down on a scrap of University paper in the Senate room. It was the meeting before he went to Perkin's —just before his troubles began !

Professor Higginson felt for that scrap of paper intuitively in the watch pocket of his waistcoat. He could carry such things there for days. It was not in the watch pocket of his waistcoat.

He searched in all the pockets of the suit he was wearing. One puts things which one is in the habit of carrying instinctively into a pocket, and one often does not remember when one did it—especially if one is given to lapses of The Primary Consciousness and Subliminal Thingumbobs !

By a process only too familiar to the less fortunate members of the professional classes, he fingered carefully every edge of the pocket lining until he found a large hole, whereat he as carefully explored all the vague emptiness of the lining beneath, and as he explored it he began to worry, for there was nothing there. Then the Professor of Subliminal Psychology suddenly remembered ! He had taken it out when he dressed that evening for Perkin's. He had put it on to the dressing table. He remembered the white paper on the white cloth, and he remembered telling himself not to forget it. He had put it into the pocket—the waistcoat pocket—of his one evening suit.

He went through that one suit very thoroughly. He found nothing. He thought he might have dropped it when he last changed. He stretched upon the floor and, lighting matches with infinite difficulty, he peered under the bed and under the wardrobe, examining every inch of the worn Brussels carpet. Not a scrap of paper appeared.

Then—suddenly—he got a touch of nausea. It was borne in upon him more and more certainly that the last time he had carried that memorandum —and worn that suit—was at Perkin's party, *and the days that followed and the nights*. That bit of paper must have dropped during one of his struggles or one of his athletic feats in the Accursed House ! That gave the matter a very new importance. If that ill-omened scrap were still in the empty house ! . . . Worse still, supposing someone had found it ? . . . It was a clue.

Professor Higginson lost no time. He took the tram, and when he reached the end of it, with infinite precautions of looking to right and left, pretending to go down side lanes, lingering at gates, he managed at last to comfort himself with the assurance that no one watched him—as indeed no one did. Every inch was, for him, alive with spies, and he exaggerated the importance of his movements, for he was a Don.

An hour or so after he had left the town he saw the neglected shrubs, the rotting gate, the beweeded gravel path ; and, standing up gaunt and terrible before him, the Accursed House within its wasted grounds.

He went up stealthily to the door. It was locked. Still gazing over his shoulder with nervous precaution, he made an effort to find some postern, but the high wall was blind everywhere, and the courtyard at the back was enclosed upon all sides.

With a confused but terrible recollection of some tag which tells us that no man falls at once to the lowest depths of turpitude, and with a sigh for the relic of his honour, he tried one of the great front windows. It was fast.

Then Lucifer once again inspired that unhappy man with cunning beyond his own. He whipped out a pocket-knife, opened the thin blade, inserted it in the crack of the sash and began to tamper, yes, to tamper, with the catch. He felt it giving, as he pushed gently and with infinite care lest any sound should betray him, when his heart suddenly stopped beating, and his blood ran dead cold, at the sound of a voice just behind him delivering this summons—

" What yer at ? "

He dropped the knife and leapt round. A sturdy fellow, short and thick-set, clothed in old bargee trousers and a pea-jacket, and with that face of labour which the police call " villainous " in their reports, was watching him unmoved.

" What yer at ? " repeated the badly-shaven lips.

" I—I was making an experiment," said Professor Higginson at random.

" Yer was," said the thick-set man, and spat. " And now yer 'll cut."

Professor Higginson was dignified.

" My good man," he said ——

" None o' that," said the good man, advancing his face in an ugly fashion ; " I 'll let yer know I 'm the caretaker. Ook it. If there was a copper in this Sahary Desert I'd put him on yer for a twofer."

Now a "twofer" is an insignificant cigar, of which two are sold for a penny; but though Professor Higginson did not know this, he understood the general drift of the remark, and he slowly began to edge away.

"I've a mind," said the pea-jacketed one, following him growling to the gate, "to tell Mr. Kirby."

"Mr. who?" said Professor Higginson eagerly.

"Mr. Kirby," repeated the man, sullenly. "It's his job this house is."

Professor Higginson felt in his trouser pocket and produced a florin. The caretaker took it, though it only confirmed his suspicions.

"Is that the name of the agent for this house? Could I get an order from him? I want to look for—I mean I want to get inside!"

"Yus! Yer do!" said the man. Then: "That's the name of Mr. Kirby, and if yer've sense yer'll get to his orfices afore me."

It was a plain hint, but Professor Higginson was not grateful. He was considering what advantage this information was to him, and as he slowly considered it he at last clearly grasped that advantage. He would be back at that house within three hours: back with the key and an order to view. And it would go hard with him if he did not find that dangerous scrap of paper. He had not wasted his florin.

"Thank you," he said rapidly, and was gone.

He reached the tram again before it was mid-afternoon. Once in the town he looked up a

directory in a shop, found Kirby and Blake's direction,
and made his way at once to that office.

Mr. Kirby had come in just an hour before. He
had sat drawing caricatures on blotting-paper with
stubs of pencil, or gazing at the ceiling. He had
written private letters with his own hand, and
addressed to people who had no known connection
with the firm, and he seemed to have attached
himself thus to his business premises, during that
one exceptional afternoon, for the advantage of
seclusion and of the telephone more than of anything
else. Moreover, he had asked peevishly once or
twice whether such and such a one had rung him up
or called for him.

When, therefore, Professor Higginson came into
the office and asked whether he could see Mr. Kirby,
said the clerk to him, " Certainly, sir," and showed
him into a room where bound copies of *Punch* and
a *Graphic* three years old, also a list of bankrupts,
beguiled the leisure of clients as they waited their turn.

" Will you send up your card ? " added the clerk
innocently.

" No," worried and feebled the Philosopher—he
had no card—" say it is Professor Higginson, and
that he wants to see Mr. Kirby most particularly."

" Is Mr. Kirby expecting you ? " continued the clerk.

" How should I know ? " said Mr. Higginson half
savagely. And the mystified young man was more
mystified still when, on giving the name to his
employer, that employer jumped up and beamed
as though he had been left a legacy, or had heard
of a dear friend's return from the dead.

" Oh, show him up ! " he said merrily. " Show

him up ! Show him up at once ! " and the chief of that great business went half-way to the door to meet his visitor.

He took him warmly by both hands as he bade him be seated. He asked in the most concerned way about his present state of health, after the terrible adventure which was now the talk of thousands. He hoped that the heat of the room with its blazing fire was not inimical to the Professor's convalescence.

Professor Higginson was rather curt for such a genial host.

" I won't detain you, Mr. Kirby," he said, " it is very good of you to have given me a moment or two of your valuable time." He thought a moment. He was not good at plots, or rather he had had to construct too many lately in too short a time. At last he began tentatively ——

" Perhaps you know, Mr. Kirby—I am afraid it is widely known—in fact, you *do* know, for you have just told me as much—that I—that in fact I have had an unfortunate—er—lapse."

Mr. Kirby nodded sympathetically.

" Pray do not insist, my dear Professor," he murmured ; " most touching, most interesting. Now with your expert knowledge of the phenomena of consciousness —— "

Professor Higginson interrupted.

" The point is, Mr. Kirby, that knowing you to be in touch with the—what shall I say—the residence business —— "

" Yes ? " said Mr. Kirby, with a polite inflection.

" Well, the fact is," blurted out the Philosopher, " my case presents a point of the highest possible interest, the highest possible scientific interest, in which you might help me. It is about a house." And here the Professor stopped dead.

Mr. Kirby watched him with crossed legs, joined finger-tips, and a very hierarchical expression.

Professor Higginson continued—

" I have an instinct, purely subliminal, mind you" (Mr. Kirby nodded, but never took his eyes off the Professor's face, and the Professor's eyes on their side never left the floor), " purely subliminal, but a strong instinct that during those days I was—I saw —no, I mean I was spiritually present in a *House*— a sort of, well, *House !*" Mr. Kirby nodded again. " I—I—I had a sort of dream —— "

" Wait a moment, Professor," said Mr. Kirby respectfully, " we must get all this quite clear. At first I understood that your complete loss of memory involved a breach in the continuity of consciousness —a blank as it were. I read all the reports, of course " (his tone was profoundly reverent), " and I will not trespass upon sacred things. But at *first* there was a blank, was there not ? "

Professor Higginson put on his lecturing tone. " We are using technical terms, my dear sir," he said in a somewhat superior manner, " indeed, highly technical terms. Primary consciousness I certainly lost. I think I may go so far as to say that I am unaware of any action of secondary consciousness." Mr. Kirby still nodded gravely, following every word. " But *subliminal consciousness* is a very different matter ! That, my dear sir," continued the Professor, smiling awkwardly, " is my own department as it were. Now the subliminal consciousness is peculiarly active in dreams, and I certainly did have a very vivid dream."

" But if your memory was wrong," said Mr. Kirby with a calculatedly puzzled look, " I mean if your memory failed about it —— "

The Professor shook his head impatiently.

" You don't understand," he said. " Please let us be clear. There's no question of memory at all."

" Not at all, not at all," said Mr. Kirby politely, " only a dream."

" It was a vision—a high vision," said the Philosopher. " I recollect some things clearly. A sort of studio roof. A big sort of skylight window. I remember that. Now of course I never can have been in such a house," continued Professor Higginson. " It's one of the first laws of subliminal consciousness that impressions are conveyed from one centre to another, transversely as it were, and not either directly or in the ordinary line from a superior to an inferior plane. To put it conversationally, not from above to below, nor from below to above. Hum ! "

" Of course ! " said Mr. Kirby. " Naturally. Quite clear."

" The whole theory of telepathy depends upon that," went on Professor Higginson, glancing up cautiously at the lawyer and dropping his eyes again.

" It could depend on nothing else," said Mr. Kirby gracefully.

" Well, you see," said the Psychologist, " I wasn't in the house, that's quite certain ; I had and have no *objective* knowledge of the house. Every psychologist of repute will bear evidence to that. It's the mere A B C of the science."

7 *

" Your reputation," said Mr. Kirby, " would weigh more than that of any colleague," and the Professor was gratified.

" You understand clearly," went on Mr. Higginson. " I never was in that house—yet I am certain such a house exists, and—well—for reasons that are very private—it is really of interest to me to discover where it may be, for though my science assures me that I had no sort of physical connection with it during that extraordinary experience, yet I am confident that its connections, inhabitants or owners, will give me a clue to what is now the chief interest of my life—and I may add, I hope without boasting, now one of the chief subjects before scientific Europe. In the interest of Science I should *see* that house. I should visit it . . . Soon. Indeed, to-day. . . . I wonder if you can help me ? . . . The house looked north," he continued abruptly, shutting his eyes and groping with his hands to add a wizard effect to the jerky sentences. " There was a drive up to it with laurel bushes, a rather weedy drive. There were four stone steps to the door, I remember those steps well, and—oh ! there was a lower ground-floor room with one window looking on to a backyard. . . . If I can find that house and have an order from its owner to visit it I shall be profoundly grateful—I thought you might help me."

" I 've got it all down," said Mr. Kirby, scribbling hurriedly, " and I will certainly find it for you. The cause of Science, Professor Higginson, is a sacred cause."

" If you *can !*—oh ! if you *can* get me an order *now*, *to-day !* " burst out the Professor, opening his

eyes suddenly and cutting short in his desperation.
" I—I—well, I should like to look over that house.
It would be of the highest possible scientific interest.
Can you," he added nervously, and as though he was
in a hurry to catch a train or something of that sort,
" can you let me have the keys—now ? "

" My dear sir," said Mr. Kirby, looking up gently,
" my dear sir, I really cannot yet be certain what
house it may be, nor whether our firm are the agents
for it, nor even whether it 's to let, though I think
it may be one I have in my mind."

He glanced at his notes again.

" Oh, yes, your firm are the agents," said the
Professor eagerly, and then added, suddenly appreciating that he was giving himself away, " I
remember receiving with extraordinary vividness
during that curious vision the spiritual impress that
your firm were the agents."

Mr. Kirby said nothing and looked nothing, and
the Professor eagerly went on to cover his tracks—

" You must know that in these purely subliminal
phenomena there is a marvellous sense of the
atmosphere, of the—er—*connotations* of the locality
—the dream locality."

" Well," began Mr. Kirby slowly, " of course, we
could not refuse you, Professor Higginson, in a
matter of such high scientific importance. . . .
We *might* have to get the leave of the owner, but in
the normal course of things we could let you look
over it, only, you see," he went on with a puzzled
expression, " you really haven't told me enough to
fix me yet as to what house it can be. . . . We
have so many to remember," he mused. . . . " It

is a peculiar sort of a house. Unfurnished, I think you said ? " he continued, looking at his notes, " except on the top floor, where there was a studio. Now, Professor," and here he looked suddenly at his visitor, " can't you recollect any other detail, some sort of faint impression ? "

" N—no," said Professor Higginson timidly. " You must remember the circumstances were extraordinarily —— "

" For instance," said Mr. Kirby imperturbably, " have you any recollection of where the bed was ? Was it in a sort of little dark room beyond the studio ? It is an extraordinary thing," he continued, pulling up his sock as he said it, " that one cannot keep one's sock up on one's leg without those horrible little garters, which I for one will *not* wear."

" Now you suggest it," said Professor Higginson slowly and with something of the feeling that a mule may have when it feels the drag on the rope, " now you suggest it I *have* a recollection of something of the sort. . . . And by the way, I seem also to remember a delicious heavenly music."

" Ah ! " said Mr. Kirby, and he gazed at a point on the carpet about eleven feet away, " wonderful thing music, only seven notes, and see what a lot you can get out of 'em ! I will smoke a cigar if you don't mind," and he lit one. " Now, were there three chairs in the room, and do you remember anything of a rope ? " said Mr. Kirby.

" I 'm not—quite—sure—about—the rope," lied Professor Higginson, pausing between every word, " but the chairs ? Ye—es ! I think I *did* see chairs —wooden chairs."

" And was the skylight broken ? "

" No—yes—possibly—very probably," floundered
the Philosopher.

" Then I 've got it," said Mr. Kirby briskly,
" I 've spotted it ! You were *quite* right when you
said you 'd never been there in the flesh. At least,
I don't think you ever can have been there. It
isn't in this town at all. It isn't in England. It 's
a place my firm looks after in the Hebrides—wonderful old place, you know—deserted. A Manse it
was. Now the history of that house —— " he was
continuing volubly, when the Professor checked
him.

" Not at all ! Not at all ! " he said angrily, " I
tell you it is somewhere close by here ! In
Ormeston ! "

" My dear sir ! " said Mr. Kirby, opening wide
eyes, " how can you know that a duplicate of the
house I am thinking of —— ? "

" I 've told you already," snapped Higginson.
" In these visions one has connotations of atmosphere,
and so on."

" Well," said Mr. Kirby, after that outburst,
shaking his head slowly from side to side, " then
I 'm of no use, none at all. I do know by chance
that place in the Hebrides, saw it only last year.
Doing it to oblige a cousin. Would have been most
interesting, most interesting, if it had been *that*.
Don't you think it *could* be that ? They 're full of
second sight in those parts."

" No," said Professor Higginson, rising with
determination and in some anger, " no, I do not think
it could be that."

"Well, then," said Mr. Kirby hopelessly, "I don't see how I can help you. Don't you think two connotations may have got mixed up?"

"No, I don't," said the Professor shortly, more and more possessed of the feeling that things were going wrong with him. "I *don't* think so. It's impossible. These things have their laws, sir, just as nature has, I mean ordinary nature, common nature, what we—er—call Natural Laws."

Mr. Kirby nodded agreeably.

"I don't think," went on Professor Higginson, "that I ought to take up any more of your time."

"Oh, but I should particularly like to hear more," said Mr. Kirby with enthusiasm.

"I'm afraid it's no use," said Professor Higginson, and he made to go out.

He was actually at the door, when Mr. Kirby added—

"Professor Higginson, I've half promised some friends to ask you to dine in London after your lecture. It was a great liberty—but they knew I lived in Ormeston. I wonder whether I might presume? Shall I drop you a line? It's the Rockingham. I might tell you something then. I might find out."

"Yes," said Professor Higginson with no enthusiasm, but he badly wanted to see that house and search it for that haunting scrap of paper, and he didn't want to lose touch with the Order to View, "yes, by all means."

"You see," added Mr. Kirby apologetically, "by the time you come to dine with me in London on Wednesday I might be able to suggest a lot of things

—an almost unfurnished downstairs room with a big deal table in it, and oaken stairs, uncarpeted, and, oh ! all the sort of things that you would expect in a house of that kind."

" Yes," said Professor Higginson, flabbergasted.

" Well, well," said Mr. Kirby more cheerfully, and shaking him cordially by the hand, " I won't keep you ; next Wednesday in town ! I 'll write ! " and he sauntered back into his room.

The great Psychologist slowly paced the street outside, then despair gave him relief, and he went home to bed.

CHAPTER XIV

In which, incredible as it may seem, a non-Pole has the better of a Pole

ON Tuesday morning Mr. Kirby woke eager for action. Things were fitting in. It was great fun.

Mr. Kirby loved to fit things in—he ought to have been a soldier.

He calculated with a pleasing exactitude. That morning — thanks to the stupid police and the telephone—he would find the Green Overcoat ; that afternoon and evening he would invite such other guests as pleased him to dine with him next day, the Wednesday, in London, after Professor Higginson's great lecture upon the Immortality of the Soul. It was an interesting subject, the Immortality of the Soul.

To make certain that all his guests should be

there, he would try to talk to one of them in London over the telephone from Ormeston that night. . . . One of them called James McAuley. He liked the boy. While he was about it he thought he would get a friend of McAuley's to come as well. He didn't know the name of the friend, but no matter; one should always ask one's friends' friends.

So deciding, Mr. Kirby, delighted at the brightness of the day, walked merrily towards a quarter of Ormeston which we have already visited, and which is not the choice of the rich. He walked through the dirty, narrow little streets, prim in his excellent kit, well-groomed and flourishing. He was old-fashioned enough to have a flower in his button-hole, and he had been very careful with his hat. He was going to see someone he knew, someone he had known professionally in the past, and with whom a few years ago he had had very interesting business. He was going to see a man who bore a fine old crusading name, but who must have come down somewhat in the world, though doubtless he had kept his family pride. He was going to see a Mr. Montague.

He knocked at the door in a sharp, commanding sort of way. It was opened quickly, and the little old figure appeared within, armed with insolence. When the eyes recognised Mr. Kirby, the face of that little old figure turned in a moment from insolence to servility.

"Good morning, Samuel," said Mr. Kirby briskly. "No, I won't come in, thank you. I only want you to tell me something. I'm sorry to trouble you. Where's that Green Overcoat of Mr. Brassington's?"

He lost it a few days ago, and a friend of mine told me that you were quite likely to know."

I will waste neither my time nor the reader's in describing Mr. Montague's face at hearing this question ; but I will say this much, that it looked like one of those faces carved in hard stone, which antiquity has left us, quite white, not expressionless, but with an expression concealed, and as one might swear, dumb. But the face spoke. It said in a very unnatural voice, a voice lacking breadth—

"I swear to God I don't know, Mr. Kirby. If I knew, I swear to God I 'd tell you."

"Just tell me what you did with it," said Mr. Kirby easily and rapidly, looking at his watch. "I 've got to fit a lot of things in."

"I swear to God, sir," said the face, "I gave it away."

Mr. Kirby's smile grew stronger, then suddenly ceased. He believed him.

"Was that all, Samuel ? " he asked, turning to go. There was a grave suggestion of peril in his voice.

The face said only—

"Well, I had to warn my own lot, Mr. Kirby ; I had to warn my nephew, sir. I had to warn Lipsky not to touch it, not touch it on any account, Mr. Kirby ! "

"Lipsky in the Lydgate ? " said Mr. Kirby. "Then he 's got it ! Good morning, Samuel," and the lawyer strode away.

He was sorry to have gone out of his way by a quarter of a mile, but he was glad to have got the information he desired.

The little closed shop in the Lydgate seemed to have something deserted about it as he came near. Mr. Kirby was familiar with the stack of old suits outside, the big placarded prices, the occasional announcements of a sale. To-day things seemed less promising and less vivacious, as though the master's hand were not there. Mr. Kirby had known that master also in the past—all in the way of business— and if anything had happened to him he would have regretted it like the passing of a landmark. He walked straight into the shop, and there, instead of the Pole Lipsky, what he saw was an obvious non-Pole, an inept Midland youth with flaxen hair, a stammerer, and a very bad salesman.

Mr. Kirby addressed his young compatriot quickly but courteously.

"Would you be kind enough to give me Mr. Brassington's Green Overcoat?" he said.

"Wh-wh-wh-what?" said the non-Pole, utterly at sea.

There is a type in the modern world which is not destined to commercial success, and certain forms of the non-Polish type present extreme examples of the kind.

"Mr. Brassington's Green Overcoat," repeated Mr. Kirby steadily and hard.

Upstairs Lipsky, rising from his sick bed, heard. He heard the unusual voice, he heard the name, and, as I have written some pages back, he came down.

There is always a common bond between intelligence and intelligence, though the intelligence of the one man be that of an Englishman and of the other

man be that of a Pole ; and as Lipsky entered the
shop Mr. Kirby and he at once picked up com-
munications, and the assistant at once dropped out
of the scheme.

"Oh, Mr. Lipsky," said Mr. Kirby courteously,
"I 'm afraid you 've been ill ! I 'm sorry for that !
But the fact is I 'm rather in a hurry, and have come
for Mr. Brassington's Green Overcoat."

"Yes, Mr. Kirby, certainly," said the shopkeeper.

He did not understand this race which was not
his, but he knew perfectly well that Mr. Kirby
would not betray him.

"Very glad you 've called, Mr. Kirby. I just got
it done up to send round to Mr. Brassington's this
minute. My assistant took it in, sir."

"I ——" began the non-Pole.

"Silence !" thundered Mr. Kirby to his compatriot, and Mr. Lipsky was very grateful.

Mr. Lipsky continued eagerly—

"You 'll find it all right, Mr. Kirby. There 's the
cheque book in the pocket, that 's how I knew it !"

"Yes, of course," said Mr. Kirby airily, "that 's
all right."

"You won't take it, Mr. Kirby," said Mr. Lipsky
respectfully ; "I 'll have it sent."

"Yes, certainly," nodded Mr. Kirby, as he went out
of the shop. "No hurry, any time this afternoon—
to my private house, not my office, you know."

Mr. Lipsky came to the door and smiled him out—
such a smile ! Yes, Mr. Lipsky knew that private
house of Mr. Kirby's ! He had been granted two or
three interviews there. He knew it extraordinarily
well.

The lawyer went back through the sunlit streets at a loose end. He felt unusually leisured, though he was a leisured man. Like the peri in the poem, his task was done.

He basked through that afternoon. He rang up the Rockingham Hotel in London to reserve a room and to order dinner for the next day. He rang up his friend Brassington again, to be sure of the appointment, and to be sure that Brassington was bringing his son. Then, when evening came, he took down the big London telephone book and looked up the number of Sir Alexander McAuley, the great doctor. It was years since Mr. Kirby had seen him; but they had known each other well in the past, and he would not mind the liberty. Besides which, what Mr. Kirby wanted as he called up Trunks after dinner that Tuesday evening was not Sir Alexander, but his son, Mr. James. Time pressed, and Mr. Kirby was very keen on talking to Mr. James McAuley.

He got Sir Alexander's house. He heard that Mr. James McAuley was out. He got the name of the restaurant where the youth was dining with some friends. He rang up that restaurant, and at last, a little after half-past nine, he had the pleasure of hearing Jimmy's fresh voice at the end of the wire.

What that conversation was I must, in my next chapter, take the reader to the other end of the wire to inform him; but hardly had he put down the receiver when the door-bell rang and the non-Pole, carrying a bundle for Mr. Kirby, appeared in the hall. Evidently Mr. Lipsky was a good business man. He would not disturb the routine of his shop; things that did not belong to business hours he did outside business hours, and he knew how to get the most out of his assistant's time.

There stood in Mr. Kirby's study a large ottoman. He lifted the lid of that Victorian piece of furniture, and bid the boy put the bundle in.

Mr. Kirby was wholly devoid of superstition. None the less, he went out of the house shortly after, and during the hour or two at his disposal he took the Midland air. Of course, there was nothing in Mr. Brassington's private twist about Green Overcoats, but why should a sensible man run any risks at all ?

CHAPTER XV

In which three young men eat, and not only eat,
but drink

THERE are few restaurants left in London where gentlemen may meet with some sort of privacy and with the chance of eating reasonable food. It might be more accurate to say there are none. But whether there are any left or not, I am going to invent one for the purposes of this story, and to inform you that on this same Tuesday night upon which Mr. Kirby was telephoning to Sir Alexander McAuley, Jimmy and Melba were very kindly entertaining Algernon Sawby Leonidas Brassington —Mr. Brassington, Jun., for short—at dinner in a private room at Bolter's.

Bolter's, I need hardly inform such a woman of the world as my reader, is the one place left in London where a man can dine well and yet at his ease. It

stands in a little street off Regent Street eastward,
and by a happy accident has been worthy of its
reputation for seventy years. Either it has not
paid Bolter's, or Bolter's has been too proud, but
anyhow the Whelps of the Lion are quite ignorant of
Bolter's, so are the cousins of the noble beast, so
certainly are the greater part of such degraded
natives of the European Continent as we permit to
visit our Metropolis and to stare at our Imperial
Populace.

Even the young bloods for the most part have not
heard of Bolter's, and as it never spends a penny
on advertisements, its name, on the rare occasions
when it appears in an article or a letter, is ruthlessly
struck out in proof by the blue pencil of the editor.

Bolter's is known and loved by perhaps two
hundred families. It is a tradition, and as you
may well imagine, enormously expensive. If you
are two dining at Bolter's, you may expect to spend
£7, and if you are three, £10. If you are very rich,
it is worth your while to dine at Bolter's. If you
are only moderately rich, it is worth your while. If
you are poor, it is also worth your while to go to
prison for not paying—so excellent is the food.

All this I tell the reader in order that he may know
how and why Jimmy and Melba were entertaining
their friend. That friend, though his father was a
very wealthy man, was a little awed by the surroundings. He had heard of Bolter's—once or
twice, not more—from the fringes of that governing
world in which some of his University friends lived.
He remembered the son of a Cabinet Minister
complaining of Bolter's, and a peer of the realm (a

former furniture dealer and picture broker and for
that matter money-lender) saying that Bolter's was
filthy. Such praise was praise indeed. He remembered that ladies did not go to Bolter's. He
remembered talk of a dinner at Bolter's just before
a little group of men had gone out in his first year to
India, and now that he was sitting in Bolter's he felt
duly impressed. He knew that Jimmy's people
were " in " what he could never be " in." Melba
was more of an enigma to him, but anyhow Melba
was thick with Jimmy and Jimmy's lot. In other
words, he knew that Jimmy and Melba were both on
the right side of a certain line which runs round very
definitely through the core of English society and
encloses a very narrow central space ; but, on the
other hand, he knew—he had the best of reasons for
knowing—that they were not exactly *flush*. He
knew they *couldn't* be flush because whereas he,
Leonidas, had in the past won £1,800 off them at
cards—and spent it—they, Jimmy and Melba, had
won £2,000 off *him*—and had never got it ! For
his father (unlike *their* fathers) had refused to pay.
But Mr. Brassington, Jun., was not the man to
introduce a subject of that kind. It is a subject of
the kind that jars on toffs, unless indeed the toffs
themselves introduce it. And on this particular
occasion they did.

Mr. Brassington, Jun., had drunk reasonably,
Jimmy largely, Melba immoderately. They had
come to that one of the many courses which consisted
in a very small frozen bird, when Jimmy playfully
threw a bone at his guest (who ducked and missed
it), and followed his action with the words.

" You didn't think we should run to this, did
you, Booby ? "

" Well," said Algernon Sawby Leonidas Brassington
delicately, " of course, I knew that you wanted me
to settle, and God knows I tried."

" That's all right," said Melba, in a voice still
clear and articulate. " Your father's paid."

And having said this, he burst into somewhat
unreasoning laughter, choked, and drank a large
tumbler of wine to cure his choking.

Booby was bewildered.

" My . . . father's . . . paid ? " he said
slowly.

Jimmy nodded to confirm the great truth.

" Touched last week, Booby," he said.

" Where ? " wondered the astonished Booby.

" At the bank," said Melba, and Jimmy added,
" Oddly enough."

" Not the whole thing ? " said Booby, his face
changing in expression as he said it.

Melba's mouth being full for the moment, he did
no more than lift up his eyes, nod and grunt.   Jimmy,
who was occupied in a swill, put down the inebriant,
drew a breath, and said—

" The whole boodle ! "

It was perhaps well for the two young men
principally concerned that they were rapidly getting
drunk, for in early youth the vice of drunkenness,
so fatal to maturer years, will often lead to astonishing
virtues.   And long before they came to the cheese
Jimmy and Melba had discovered that they must
talk of the matter seriously.   Indeed, Jimmy verged
on the sentimental, Melba upon the stupidly pompous,

as the ordeal approached. It was over coffee that they faced it, and brandy was their aid.

"Look here, Booby," said Jimmy, after he and Melba had spent a silent five minutes mentally egging each other on, "you ought to know the truth, it's only fair. We *made* your father sign."

Algernon Sawby Leonidas Brassington had a sudden retrospective vision of his father, and he could make no sense out of the words.

"You *made* him?" he said, flushing a little. "Cursed if you did! He'd make *you* more like!"

An illogical phrase enough, but one sufficiently full of meaning.

"Possibly," said Jimmy, with the insulted dignity of a person who has dined. "If you don't want to hear about it you needn't."

"Shut up, Jimmy," said Melba diplomatically.

He tried to make his high and now uncertain voice kind as he went on to the younger Mr. Brassington—

"You see, Booby, it's like this. Th' was a lillel comprulsion—y' know. There was scene, wasn't there, Jimmy?"

"Oh, yes, scene right 'nough!" said Jimmy.

"Well, anyhow, he gave us the cheque, and then; you know, we had to prevent its getting out—his getting out, I mean."

"I don't understand a word you say," said Booby.

"No," said Jimmy too thoughtfully, glaring at the fire. "We were 'fraid that."

"If there's a row, Booby," said Melba affectionately, "if there's real row, y' ought to be warned. That's what we think."

"That's it," said Jimmy.

Then under the impression that their ordeal was over and their duty done, the two conspirators lapsed into silence. It was a silence which might have lasted some minutes.

It was broken by the ringing of an electric bell in the corridor outside, a sound muffled by the door, and the German reservist whom his unscrupulous Government secretly paid to wait at table at Bolter's, came in to tell Mr. McAuley that he was wanted at the telephone.

The god Bacchus, when he came out of Asia with those panthers of his, came into Europe the master of many moods, and Jimmy was a young man careless and content as he lifted the receiver. He heard a clear and rather high voice ask him whether he was Mr. McAuley. It was a voice he seemed to remember. It was the voice of Mr. Kirby.

" I asked them at home where you were," said the voice, " and they told me I should find you if I rang up Bolter's."

" Thank you," said Jimmy too loudly—but he had no cause for gratitude !

" I am talking from Ormeston," said the voice ; " my name is Kirby."

Jimmy's mood began to change.

" I 've asked for six minutes," the voice went on, " but I may as well tell you at once. It 's about that house you took—Greystones. Now, Mr. McAuley, in your own interests, would you be good enough to take the 10.15 from King's Cross. I 'll meet you at Ormeston Station."

The very brief heroic mood not unknown to the god Bacchus now rushed over Jimmy.

"Upon my word, sir!" he began. Then in the twinkling of an eye another mood—one of alarm— prompted him to add, "Is it anything really urgent?" And his third mood was panic.

Good Lord! He could imagine one or two terribly urgent things in connection with Greystones. What if old Brassington were lying there dead? What if he had exploded, and told the police in spite of his own shame?

"Mr. Kirby!" he cried in a changed voice into the little black cup, "Mr. Kirby!" The wire was dumb, there was only the buzzing and spitting and little fiendish snarls which the marvellous invention has added to modern life. "Mr. Kirby!" said Jimmy still higher and for the third time, but it was a woman's voice that answered—

"Another three minutes?" it said snappishly, and then the wire went dead.

Twice more and once again did poor Jimmy implore the voice, but Mr. Kirby knew the nature of man, especially of youthful man. He had not attempted to persuade. In the study of his own house at Ormeston he had already replaced the receiver, and was taking down from the book-shelf a volume of Molière. He loved that author, and there was a good two hours before he need meet the night mail at the station.

After a quarrel with the clerk-in-charge and sundry foolish troubles, Jimmy abandoned the machine. He came back to his two companions. They were in the thick of some silly vinous argument or other. They looked up at his entry, and they saw that he was changed.

"What's matter, Jimmy?" said Melba.

" I—I—I want to talk to you," said Jimmy nervously, and singularly sober. He looked at Booby.

" Oh, don't mind me," said Booby.

" Well, but we do," said Jimmy ruefully, and he drew Melba into the passage outside.

" There 's a row up," he said.

" What about ? " said Melba.

"Old Brassington," said Jimmy in a nervous whisper.

" Peached ? He wouldn't dare," whispered Melba incredulously.

" Why not ? " said Jimmy, agonised. " I 've been called, you know. Called up from Ormeston. Urgently. By the lawyer. There 's a thing in the law, Melba, called ' duress.' "

" Oh, rats ! He can't prove anything ! "

" Damn it all ! " said Jimmy, " we don't know that."

" He wouldn't make a fool of himself," continued Melba uncomfortably.

" You can't ever tell with these old jossers. Anyhow, that lawyer chap my father knows, the man we got the house from, has rung me up, and I 've got to go and see him in Ormeston to-night by the 10.15."

Melba said nothing.

" Would you go ? " continued Jimmy, seeking valiance from his friend.

" No," said Melba stoutly.

" 'Tisn't you that have got to do it," said Jimmy bitterly. " 'Twas me he called up. I signed, you know, Melba. It 's *my* name they 've got."

" If it was me—— " began Melba.

" 'Tisn't you," said Jimmy rudely, and as he said it Booby came out.

"If you two are going to talk business," he said suspiciously, "I'm going home to my rooms."

"Fact is, Booby," said Jimmy, "I've just heard about my aunt; she's dying."

Booby was concerned.

"Oh, dear!" he said.

"Yes," went on Jimmy rapidly, bringing out his watch, and seeing that it lacked only seven minutes of ten, "it's bad, very bad! I can't wait."

He thrust himself into his coat, looked over his shoulder as he ran down the stairs, and with the very disconcerting cry, "Keep Booby!" hurled at his companion, he sought the street and a taxi, and was half-way to King's Cross before he remembered that Melba must pay for the dinner. But the thought was small comfort compared with the trial that was before him. And for an hour and three-quarters as the train raced up north to the Midlands he comforted himself less and less at the prospect.

CHAPTER XVI

In which cross-examination is conducted " en échelon," and if you don't know what that means I can't help you

CHEERFUL, more than cheerful, all smiles, Mr. Kirby was standing at midnight upon the arrival platform of the great station at Ormeston as the night mail came in. He saw the slender figure of a young man whose every gesture betrayed an absurd anxiety coming bewildered up from the end of the train, and looking about him as though seeking a face.

It was a fine cordial welcome that greeted James McAuley, not in the least what he had expected. He was enormously relieved.

"My dear Mr. McAuley," said the lawyer, with a fine generosity of impulse and in the heartiest of tones, "how very good of you to come! I confess I was very much in doubt whether you would understand the urgency of my message at such short notice. You see," he added, lying expansively, "they cut us off."

"Yes," said Jimmy, thinking that explained all.

"It was a terrible nuisance," pattered on Mr. Kirby, as he led the boy outside to a cab; "that's the worst of the telephone. It's a great help in one way, but . . . Why, you haven't brought a bag!"

"No," said Jimmy. "I shall go back by the night mail."

"As you will, my dear sir," said the lawyer.

He gave the address of his house, and they drove off.

When they got into the study and were served with drink, Jimmy remembered his anxieties. He considered that imperative message and that hurried journey. The business must be very urgent indeed. He was the more certain of it as he watched Mr. Kirby's face change to an expression more settled and less familiar. As Mr. Kirby said nothing, Jimmy volunteered another remark.

"I was giving young Brassington a dinner," he said. "Perhaps you know him? He was at King's with me." Mr. Kirby said nothing. "He belongs to this town," added Jimmy.

Mr. Kirby opened fire in a grave and measured voice.

"Mr. McAuley," he said, "I know that you know young Mr. Brassington."

The words seemed to have a little more meaning than Jimmy liked.

"I am an intimate friend of Mr. Brassington, Senior. We think a good deal of him in Ormeston, Mr. McAuley."

Jimmy crossed his legs, leant back in his chair, sipped his wine, and put on an unconcerned, man-of-the-world visage, not unlike that of a criminal about to be hanged.

Mr. Kirby, with his head thoughtfully poised upon the fingers of his right hand, and looking steadily away from Jimmy's face, said—

"Yes, we know Mr. Brassington, and we respect him highly."

Jimmy could bear the tension no longer.

"What is it you want to say to me about Greystones?" he said suddenly.

"Oh, yes, Greystones," said Mr. Kirby, "of course! But your mention of the Brassingtons made me turn my mind to that sad loss Mr. Brassington has had. I dare say his son told you. I am afraid he can't recover—but the bank admits it is a forgery."

"Forgery!" shrieked Jimmy.

It suddenly occurred to him that Booby's fiendish father had discovered an awfully effective line of attack.

"Well, well," said Mr. Kirby, "that's not business. Of course, I shouldn't have troubled you as I have about other people's business. But about Greystones, Mr. McAuley, the trouble is—of course, I do not blame you, but you will see you are legally responsible—well, the trouble is that after you left the place—painting, weren't you, I think?—we found the studio in—well, in an odd condition; and, you see," he went on, shifting his position, and still conversational, "between you and me, the owner of the house is a little—why, almost a little *odd*." Mr. Kirby smiled as he proceeded. "It 's not my business to talk about one client to another," he said, "but you 'll understand me. Fact is, it really sounds too ridiculous, and I did what I could to stop him; but you will understand why I telephoned. He said he 'd summons you to-morrow. He says it 's twenty-one pounds."

Jimmy heard not a word. He was thinking of vastly more important things.

Mr. Kirby continued—

"Of course, I would have paid and communicated with you afterwards. Mr. McAuley." Mr. Kirby laughed professionally. "You are legally responsible, whoever it was got in and did the harm. The time isn't up, you see, and you know the absurdity of the thing is that a man *can* issue a writ like that! Why, bless you, you can go and buy a pair of boots on credit and find the writ waiting for you when you get home! It 's ridiculous, but it 's the law."

Jimmy's face was hot and his eyes were too bright.

"It was *not* a forgery, Mr. Kirby!" he said.

"Not a what?" said Mr. Kirby, looking up with a fine affectation of confusion. "I 'm not talking about that, Mr. McAuley. Really, poor Brassington's loss is none of our business. But if you 're interested, and if you 're going to see young Brassington, you might tell him that his father 's put the whole thing

in my hands, and I am going to have details of the
cheque and who it was made out to to-morrow by
post at my office."

"Mr. Kirby," said Jimmy, in the most agitated of
voices, "I solemnly swear to God that that cheque
was not forged!"

"Really, Mr. McAuley," said Mr. Kirby, "I don't
see what you have to do with ——"

"Yes, but you *will* see," interrupted Jimmy
bitterly, "you will see. To-morrow morning!"

"Come, come," said Mr. Kirby, "I can't have all
this unofficial information. It isn't fair, you know,
not fair to my position as a lawyer. If only you 'll
let me know about that little sum for damages at
Greystones, since the landlord is so ——"

"Mr. Kirby," burst out the unfortunate James,
"the matter will not brook a moment's delay!
That cheque—Mr. Brassington's cheque, the cheque
you say was forged—was made out to me!"

"*What!*" shouted Mr. Kirby, springing to his feet.

"That cheque, Mr. Kirby," went on James firmly,
was made out to *me*. *I* passed it through the bank,
and I have that money in my bank, at least a good
deal of it, and I have paid it away—my part of it—
nearly all to my creditors."

Then he remembered again that Melba would have
to pay for the dinner, but it was very small comfort.

Mr. Kirby drew a prolonged breath.

"Really, my dear sir!" he said.

"Yes, Mr. Kirby," continued Jimmy, "to *me*.
And I have passed it into my account and I have
disbursed the money. I am not ashamed of it ; and
I will answer for it to any man. It was the payment

8

of a just debt, and *it was given to me by Mr. Brassington himself*, there ! "

" My dear Mr. McAuley," began Mr. Kirby again.

" I am telling you the plain truth, and I have witnesses who can go into the box and swear. Not all that wretched, snivelling old fellow can do ——"

" An old friend, Mr. McAuley," said Mr. Kirby suavely, " an old friend ! "

" Well," compromised Jimmy, " I will say Puritan. Not all that old Puritan's money can get over the plain facts. We can swear to it, both of us. The place and the time. It was the morning after, and it was at Greystones."

" The morning after what ? " said Mr. Kirby.

" Tuesday, the morning after that party, of course. Exactly a week ago. The date 's on the cheque, and what 's more, Mr. Kirby, I have Mr. Brassington's letter signed by him on that occasion and admitting the debt and his payment of it."

" Really," said Mr. Kirby, " indeed ! This is most astonishing."

" He was there," said Jimmy, " in that ridiculous Green Overcoat of his, and he pulled the cheque book out of his pocket. At least, it was in his pocket," corrected Jimmy, with a careful fear of tripping up over a verbal inaccuracy where the law was concerned. " He tried to get out of it, but we wouldn't have it, Mr. Kirby, and so—and so he paid."

" You are perfectly certain it was Mr. Brassington ? " said Mr. Kirby.

" No manner of doubt in the world," said Jimmy calmly. " We got him to come with us as he left the party, and we put it before him ; and as I tell you, he did hesitate, but he paid at last, and it was a just debt. I may as well tell you, Mr. Kirby, it was his son's debt. We had lost more than that to our friend in the past, and we paid honourably, and we weren't going to be welched."

"After all, Mr. McAuley," said Mr. Kirby, after a little thought, "I have asked you if you are sure it was Mr. Brassington, and the thing is important. Was he a tall, rather lanky man, with a nervous way with him and loosely dressed ? Did he thrust his hands into his pockets ? Did he try to talk about Philosophy or his being a Philosopher, or something of that sort ? Had he very large feet ? "

" Yes, I think," said Jimmy reminiscently. " Yes, he was tall and spare, and he was nervous, distinctly, even violently you might say. Yes—he had large feet, very, and he said something about being a Philosopher or Philosophy. And at *first* he had his hands in his pockets—but afterwards you know, well ——"

" Well, look here," said Mr. Kirby thoughtfully, " it was Mr. Brassington as you say—tall and spare and very nervous, and on that Philosophy crank, which is King Charles's head to him, and in that Green Overcoat of his. Oh, it must have been him all right ! But why didn't you go to his house and ask him for the cash ? What 's all this business about Greystones ? "

Jimmy kept silent. At last he said—

" That 's his business, Mr. Kirby, and he can tell you that end of the story."

" Well, look here," said Mr. Kirby, " I have really no right to get anything of this sort out of you."

" It 's the truth," said Jimmy.

"Yes, I know," said Mr. Kirby; "but you have to be starting for that night mail, and " (he mused) "I tell you what, I 'll stop that ridiculous business about Greystones in the morning. I 've got to go up to town. Do you think you could see me to-morrow in town ? What with your father's public position and Mr. Brassington's, Mr. McAuley, it 's much better to have the whole of that *other* thing out in private. Couldn't you come early and stay to dine ? "

"Yes," said Jimmy, rising to go, "I could ; but wait a minute. I have promised my father to go to a big lecture—he wants me to take my sister."

"Where ? " said Mr. Kirby carelessly.

"At the Research Club," said Jimmy. "Don't know who 's giving it. It 's about ghosts. It 'll be over by six. Where will you be stopping ? "

"I shall be at the Rockingham Hotel," said Mr. Kirby, helping the young man on with his coat as they stood at the door. It 's close to where the Research Club meets, and I 'll expect you any time from six o'clock onwards. I shan't go out. Good night," he said heartily, shaking Jimmy's hand with all the confidence in the world. " I don't understand it yet, but you 're both honourable men, and I fancy there 's been some mistake."

Jimmy reserved his opinion and went off to his train.

The lawyer went back into his study, knelt on the floor, lifted the lid of the ottoman with his right hand, put the fingers of his left upon the open under lip of that piece of furniture to steady himself, and gazed quizzically and sadly at the Green Overcoat.

"A beast !" he said. "A fate-bearing, disreputable beast ! "

But even as he said it the heavy lid slipped from the palm of his right hand. He had but just time to withdraw his left hand before it crashed down.

Mr. Kirby got up a little shakily. He was a man of imagination, and he winced internally as he thought of crushed fingers.

" Try that on again ! " he murmured, wagging his head savagely at the Green Overcoat where it basked hidden within the ottoman ; " try that on again, and I 'll rip you up ! "

With that he switched off the light and made his way to bed, maturing his plans for to-morrow. But he rather wished he had some outhouse or other in which to hide the garment. He felt a little afraid of all sorts of things—for instance, fire.

CHAPTER XVII

In which a Professor professes nothing, a Lecture is not delivered, and yet something happens

IT was the morrow Wednesday, in London, at Galton's Rooms, and near five o'clock.

Professor Higginson was feeling exceedingly nervous. He came into the little room where it was customary to receive the Lecturer when the Research Club organised one of its great functions at Galton's, and he was not over-pleased to see three gentlemen waiting for him. He had hoped there would be no one but a servant, or at the most the

secretary. He was holding a little brown bag in his
hand. It contained his MSS. and a cap and gown.
He asked whether he was to wear his cap and gown.

" O—O—ah ! I suppose so, what ? " said one
of the gentlemen who was beautifully groomed,
and had iron grey hair, and what is more wore a
single eye-glass.

" That 's all right, Biggleton, isn't it ? "

He turned to a very portly man, quite bald, who
kept his eyes so close shut that one might have
thought him blind ; but Professor Higginson knew
at that word that he was standing in the presence
of Lord Biggleton, and he suffered that mixture
of pleasure and apprehension which Dons suffer in
the presence of the great.

He wondered who the first speaker might be. If
this bald-headed man with eyes shut fast like a pig
was Lord Biggleton, why then the well-groomed
man with iron-grey hair and the single eye-glass,
who was so familiar, might be the greatest in the
land.

He was not to be informed. All old Biggleton
said was—

" What 's that, Jack ? Yes," and steadfastly
refused to open his eyes ; but Professor Higginson,.
unobservant as he was, could see that they were
not absolutely fast, but that between the upper and
the lower lid there gleamed an intense and dangerous
cunning.

It was always said that Lord Biggleton might
have had the Premiership if he had chosen, but
certainly a man with those eyes had reached whatever
eminence he cared to reach. There was no meeting

them. They lay in ambush behind the heavy lids, and did useful work through the slits beneath.

All this did not put the Professor at his ease. He pulled out his MSS. and let it drop. A third man picked it up, and handed it to him again with a ready smile. Professor Higginson on first coming into the room had taken him for a young man, for he had the cut and the facial lines of 'youth ; but as the light from the window fell upon him as he picked up the papers, the face that smiled was a face well over fifty, perhaps nearer sixty. Professor Higginson was not a little astonished to see the same smile suddenly appearing and disappearing on the face three or four times about nothing in particular, and directed towards no one. A little more experience of the world would have enabled him to label the features and the man, for that smile goes with the Ministry of the Fine Arts, and no less a one than Sir John Hooker stood before him. But Mr. Higginson had got no further than Lord Biggleton, that was enough for him !

He struggled into his gown with difficulty, and wondered whether a fourth man who helped him on was a Home Secretary or a Field-Marshal or what.

They made a little procession, Biggleton putting upon the Professor's back a powerful pushing hand by way of encouragement, the well-groomed man with the eye-glass saying " What ? " twice to himself inanely, and the Minister for the Fine Arts leading the way with a gait like a dromedary's.

They passed through a door and a lifted curtain, and came into the great room. There was a small raised platform to which the Professor was guided,

the three men walked back into the body of the hall,
and the Professor found himself alone, and without
friends, gowned, with his body of MSS. before him
upon a desk, and overlooking three or four hundred
of the richest and therefore the most powerful men
and women in England—with not a few of their
hangers-on.

In moments of strain sub-conscious impressions
are the strongest, as no one should know better
than a Professor of Psychology ; and Professor
Higginson was free to confess in later years that in
the first moments of nervous agony which he suffered
as he looked over that mass of Cabinet Ministers,
fine ladies, actresses, money-lenders, black-mailers,
courtesans and touts, the chief thing that impressed
him was the enormous size of the women's hats !

He grasped the desk firmly, cleared his throat,
and began to read.

" The hope of a life beyond the grave —— "

Here Professor Higginson lifted his head and
fumbled for a moment with his collar-stud. It was
an unfortunate, it was a tragic move ! For as he
lifted his eyes during that one instant he saw a sight
that froze his blood. Squeezing with many apologies
through the standing mass at the end and sides of
the great room was a very well-dressed young gentleman, close-knit, dark in features, an athlete, and the
features above the smart coat and collar were features
that he knew !

The form edged its way, bearing before it with
exquisite skill an exquisite top hat, inverted. It
was making for the front row of chairs, where one or
two places still remained reserved and unused, and,

as that form advanced, subliminal fear—the Oldest of the Gods—towered up over Professor Higginson's soul. It was Jimmy!

The young man had made his way to the front row of chairs ; he had sat down ; he had carefully deposited his hat beneath it. The mass of those who govern us were beginning to turn their faces, some in annoyance, some in amusement, towards him—the two duchesses, the four actresses, the eight courtesans had already lifted to their eyes long-handled spectacles of scorn, when the dreadful little silence was broken by the Professor mumbling once more mechanically with eyes staring before him his opening sentence—

" The hope of a life beyond the grave —— "

The young man had looked up and had seen the Professor's face ! The Professor had seen the sudden recognition in the young man's eyes !

That day he read no more. With a curious unformed cry, such as a hunted animal will give when it is too suddenly roused from its retreat, he snatched his papers up, stumbled down the three steps of the platform, bolted through the curtain and the door —and was off !

He was off, racing through the little ante-room, he was flying down the stone staircase three steps at a time. The Subliminal Self was out on holiday ; it was working top-notch, and Lord ! how it drove the man !

In the room thus abruptly abandoned by its principal figure there was confusion and not a little of that subdued delight with which the rich always hail some break in the monotony of their lives.

8 *

Most of the men were standing up, the less bulky
of the ladies had followed their example, perhaps
a hundred people were talking at once, when, not
thirty seconds after the Professor had performed
his singular gymnastic feat, one in that audience had
put two and two together, and had been struck by
an inspiration from heaven. And the fine frocks,
and the good coats and trousers and the top hats, and
the *lorgnettes* and the single eye-glasses got a sharp
second shock at seeing Jimmy, who had so lately
arrived, leap with the quick and practised gesture
of an athlete to the platform, cut across it like a
hare, and disappear in his turn through the curtain
and the door beyond.

He was after him ! . . . Down the long corridor
which ran along the basement of Galton's, to the side
door where professionals entered, tore the Professor.
He had reached its end, when, glancing over his
shoulder, he saw that face he would not see, and as
he passed the door-keeper he shouted in an agonised
cry, " Stop him ! " and plunged into the street.

The door-keeper was the father of a family, a
heavy drinker, and a man of peace. But for all he
knew there was a shilling in it somewhere, and he
stood up—ah, how unwisely !—to meet the charge of
that young Cambridge bone and muscle which was
thundering down the passage in pursuit.

He spread out his arms awkwardly to enforce his
message of delay, and before he knew what had
happened he was down on the stone floor, holding
desperately to something living that struggled above
him, but himself oblivious of his name and place.
As he came to, the first thing he was conscious of

was some considerable pain in the right arm upon
which he lay. The next was a sharp memory of foot-
ball in early youth, and the next was the sight of
an over-well-dressed young man holding a top hat
in his clenched hand, and sprinting a hundred yards
away up the street.

The delay had been one of only a few seconds,
but ten seconds is a hundred yards.

Jimmy saw a little knot of people running ahead.
They took a turning and were lost to him ; but
Jimmy was too eager to suffer a check. Either
Brassington was not Brassington, or there were
two Brassingtons, or there was *no* Brassington, or
pursy old merchants were Dons, or the world was
standing on its head ! But anyhow, *one man knew
the truth*, and that one man must be gripped tight,
and the truth had out of him—quick—quick !

Painful alternatives followed through Jimmy's
mind as he ran—prison, suicide, enlistment—for in
such an order of evils does luxury put the British
Army. But one obvious purpose stamped itself
upon him : the man who knew must be got hold of,
privately and securely, and must tell him all—and
must tell him soon. He picked up the scent again
from a gentleman leaning against an area railing
(who sold it for a trifling sum), and hotly followed up
his quarry—not two minutes behind.

At top speed, hatless and gowned, clutching his
notes, the tall and lanky Don careered, as might a
camel career whom some massive lion pursues in
the deserts of the East. Not often are the streets
of London afforded so great a spectacle as that of a
Philosopher, muddily splashed, gowned and hatless,

with long loose legs and wild head in air, racing with a mob at his heels.

Those Londoners who happened to be at once at leisure and unconstrained by convention—newsboys and boot-blacks, loungers, rambling thieves—pelted after him in a small but increasing crowd. Mr. Higginson heard their steps, and, what was worse, he saw amongst them a policeman. He dashed down an alley that opened to his left, turned up a court, and ran to ground with a promptitude that was amazing. For in the little court and under a dark arch of it he had seen the swing-door of a low and exceedingly ill-favoured public-house.

Once within the refuge, he sat down gasping. An elderly woman crowned with false hair was watching him severely from behind the bar as he sank, with head thrown back, and leaning upon the wooden partition attempting to recover himself. Outside he heard to his immense relief the thundering feet go past. They had missed his doubling !

Mind speaks to mind in moments of strong emotion without the medium of words. Professor Higginson recognised that unless he drank something he would be thrown to the wolves. He had never been in a public-house in his life. He had no conception of its habits. But the woman's eye was strong upon him, and he had to give an order. He gave it in this form—

" I think I should like—no, I think on the whole I should prefer a glass of, let us say, ale."

" Four Alé ? " said the woman severely.

" No, one," said Professor Higginson, whereat she fired suddenly and said—

"None of your lip, young man!" (Professor Higginson was in his fifty-seventh year, and looked it.) "None of your funny business! Who are yer, any way? I 've half a mind —— " but the thought of profit recalled her.

She had already seized the handle of the pump and drawn him his glass, when the noise of feet returned, less tumultuous, and an exceedingly unpleasing voice was saying that there was no thoroughfare. An official-sounding voice was replying with dignity, and Professor Higginson went to pieces—inwardly altogether, outwardly not a little— when he saw entering through the swing-door a policeman, a policeman who, when he looked the Philosopher up and down with due care, asked him, "What 's this?" and received no coherent reply.

"That 's what I was asking myself," said the woman with the false hair vigorously. "Come in here all of a blow, muttering, with something wicked in his eyes, as you can see. I was ordering of him out when you came in!"

Professor Higginson had exhausted that vein of invention which the Evil One had hitherto so liberally supplied. He sank upon the dirty little beer-stained stool behind him, and jibbered at the avenger of the law.

"I 've lost my memory," he said.

"Lost your *what?*" said the policeman, half threatening and half in doubt, hesitating in his venal mind between a really good cop and the disastrous results of interfering with a toff; when, before a reply could be given to so simple a query, an authoritative voice and strong step were heard together pushing through the crowd outside, and there came into the mean place the excellently dressed figure and strong young face of Jimmy.

They say that the youngest generals make the best tacticians, though sometimes the worst strategists. Jimmy acted like lightning.

" There you are ! " he said genially to Mr. Higginson —and a little shriek automatically cut itself short in the Professor's throat and ended in a gurgle.

" There you are ! " he said again, laying a powerful left hand upon Mr. Higginson's shoulder—and it was pitiful to see the Pragmatist shrink as he did so.

Jimmy turned round and gazed in a pained but authoritative way at the policeman, who instinctively touched his helmet, recognising the master-class.

" It 's my father, officer," said Jimmy, gently and sadly.

" I 'm sure," said the policeman, finding a little coin as large as a sixpence, but much more valuable, which had suddenly appeared in his great palm, " I 'm glad you 've come, sir ! I was worrying what to do ! "

" Oh, you needn't worry ! " said Jimmy kindly again ; then, with a pained look, he added, " It 's not so serious as it looks ! "

He almost broke down, but he struggled manfully, and the policeman followed him with solemn respect.

" It will be all right. It 's over-work."

He turned to Higginson and said with pathetic reverence, " Come, dad," and he exercised upon the Professor's arm so authoritative a grip that instinctively that Philosopher rose.

Conflicting doubts and fears were in that academic mind, and when the doubts and fears in the academic

mind run not in one current, then is the academic
mind so confused that it is impotent.   If he fought
or struggled he would be arrested.   If he was arrested
and in the hands of the law there might come out
at any moment   .   .   .   oh, Lord! and if he
acquiesced—what then ?   What would that young
fiend do to him ?   Where would he take him ?
Between the two he did nothing, but stood helpless
there, hating Jimmy, hating the whole organisation
of British credit, hating its cheque books and its
signatures, hating the majestic fabric of his country's
law, hating its millions, hating the wretched mass of
poverty that waited tip-toe and expectant outside,
and now and then peeped in through the swing-doors.

As Jimmy led the older man out firmly by the arm
the little mob would have followed.   But the policeman who has touched coin is a different animal from
a policeman before feeding time.   He savagely
struck at the dirty lads and frowsy women who made
up the little assembly, and cleared them off in loud
tones, aiming a violent kick which just missed the
little child who dodged it.   The gentlemen must be
left in peace.   He touched his helmet again to the
said gentlemen.   He very tactfully sauntered slowly
behind as Jimmy hurried his prize rapidly down the
alley and into the broad street outside.

A qnarter of a mile away, or a little more, the
swell crowd would be coming out of Galton's.   Five
minutes in the open street with a gowned, hatless
figure would mean another crowd.   Jimmy decided
again with admirable rapidity.

" Come into the Rockingham with me," he said,
still keeping his arm tightly linked in the Professor's.

" To the where ? " said Mr. Higginson, recognising the name. " What do you want with me ? " He was not exactly dragging back, but sending signals of resistance through the nervous gestures he made.

" Simply to talk with you ; only ten minutes, Mr. Brassington."

" I am not Brassington."

" Yes. I know. At least, I must see you for ten minutes," said Jimmy, rapidly making for the fine great portal of the Rockingham. That great portal meant safety and retreat, and it was not one hundred yards up the broad pavement.

Professor Higginson yielded. They went past the magnificent porter, through the lounge ; they were stared at a little, but no more.

Jimmy took his capture to a corner of the smoking-room, sat him down in comfort, and asked him what he drank.

The Professor, with a confused memory of a recent experience, muttered, " A little ale," but when it came he did not drink it, for ale was something which he could not touch. Jimmy, drinking brandy, spoke to him in a low tone, and with enormous earnestness.

" Professor Higginson," he began, " there 's been some bad mistake, some very bad mistake."

" I don't understand what you mean," said Professor Higginson doggedly.

" Good heavens ! " said Jimmy, really startled, and looking him full in the face. " You mean to say you don't . . ."

" I lost my memory," muttered Professor Higginson savagely, looking at the floor, " I should have thought you would have heard about it. I lost it," he said, with rising voice and passion, "after the brutal treatment —— "

"Oh, then, you remember that!" said Jimmy coolly.

"Dimly," replied the Professor through his set teeth. He was getting to feel ugly. "Very dimly. And after that my memory fails altogether."

"Well," said Jimmy, leaning back at his ease, and drinking his brandy, "I'll refresh it for you. We gave you your cheque book, Mr. Brassington——"

"I tell you my name's not Brassington," whispered the Professor in a mixture of anger and fear. "If you talk like that at the top of your voice someone'll hear you!"

"You're not Mr. Brassington?" said Jimmy, eyeing him steadily. "That's what you said on the night when you—when you lost your memory."

"Is it?" answered the Philosopher sullenly. "Then I told the truth. Damn it all, man," he said, exploding, "isn't it plain who I am? Didn't you see the people in that room? And don't you" (here a recollection of his own importance swelled him), "don't you know what my position is in the Guelph University?"

"Certainly, Professor Higginson," said Jimmy, in exactly the same tone in which he had said "Mr. Brassington" a minute before. "I quite understand. Unfortunately, during that terrible mental trouble of yours you signed something —— "

"Then it doesn't count," said Professor Higginson, shaking his head very rapidly from side to side like a dog coming out of a pond, "it doesn't count!" he said again in a still higher tone, "it doesn't count! I won't have it! I don't understand a word you say ! " and he sank back with every symptom of exhaustion.

" There 's nothing to get nervous about, Professor Higginson," said Jimmy quietly, as he leant forward to emphasise his words. " Supposing you did sign something, it wouldn't be any harm, would it ?   As a matter of fact, you signed a cheque —— "

"Doesn't count ! "said Professor Higginson, staring in front of him, and beginning to get a little yellow.

" No, of course it doesn't," said Jimmy soothingly, " but it was Mr. Brassington's cheque."

" I don't believe it ! " said Professor Higginson, still yellower, " and it doesn't count, anyhow !   I 've taken legal advice, and I know it doesn't count ! "

" Oh, you 've taken legal advice—about something you don't remember ? " said Jimmy with a curious smile. " However, it 's silly to go on like this. The point is," he added rather earnestly, " that that cheque was made out to me."

" Then I 've got you ! " said the worthy Don triumphantly, though in truth he had but the vaguest idea of how or why, but he wanted to keep his end up in general, and he thought the phrase was useful.

" Yes," said Jimmy, with a glance of quiet affection and control, " and I 've got *you ;* and what 's more, I 've got a witness. Your unfortunate loss of memory prevents your knowing that, Professor Higginson."

The Professor's lips were framing once more the ritual formula, " It doesn't count," when his eyes fixed with a horrid stare upon the short but pleasing figure of Mr. Kirby, which walked into the room, nodded genially at him, then as genially at Jimmy.

The solicitor drew up a chair and sat down before the two men.

"Didn't know you knew each other," he said in his cheerful, rather jerky voice.

"We don't" had almost framed itself on the Professor's lips, when he thought better of it, and to his horror heard Jimmy say that the Professor and he had met on board ship in the Mediterranean some years ago—and how glad he was to come across him again.

"It is a funny thing how small the world is," said Mr. Kirby simply. "You meet a man under one set of circumstances, and you get to know him quite intimately—so that you will remember him all your life—and then you think never to see him again, when he turns up quite unexpectedly, doesn't he? . . . You know Mr. Brassington?" he added genially, looking at the Professor.

"I—I—I—I know the name," said the wretched man.

"Oh, you must know the man himself," said Mr. Kirby in his heartiest manner. "He's one of the best men in your town, and he's got a particular devotion to intellectual things, you know. *You* know him, I think?" he continued, turning round to the younger man.

"Yes," said Jimmy solemnly, "yes; at least, I don't know that I ever met Mr. Brassington, but I was at college with his son, you know that, Mr. Kirby."

"You don't know him?" said Mr. Kirby, in mild astonishment. "Well, you'll be glad to meet him, he likes young men; and between you and me, *he's*

a useful kind of man to know. You know his son ?
I 'm sure he 's talked of you often enough ! I
ought to remember *that !* "

Jimmy winced. There was an interval of silence,
during which all three men were occupied apparently
with idle thoughts. It was broken by Mr. Kirby
saying, as he looked at both his acquaintances in
turn—

" Mr. Brassington and his son are in the hotel now.
I 'll go and fetch them."

CHAPTER XVIII

In which the Green Overcoat triumphs and comes home

In a couple of minutes Mr. Kirby returned. He had
Mr. Brassington closely locked by the right arm, and
was walking easily with him into the room. Booby
sheepishly followed.

" Mr. McAuley," said Mr. Kirby genially, " this is
Mr. Brassington."

Young men do not control their faces well (unless
they are the sons of scoundrels and have inherited
their fathers' talents). Jimmy looked exactly like a
man who knows nothing of the sea and has just come
to the lump on the bar.

Mr. Brassington gave a very violent movement,
which Mr. Kirby, his arm securely linked in his
friend's, checked with a wrench of iron.

" You don't know Professor Higginson, I think, do
you, Brassington ? "

He introduced the two men, and the Philosopher

knew more of the Merchant than the Merchant did of the Philosopher.

"And now," continued Mr. Kirby pleasantly, but a little pompously (it was not in his nature to be pompous, but the occasion needed it), "now we all go upstairs. I 've asked one of Mr. McAuley's friends to dinner. He is also a friend of yours, Mr. Algernon," he said, turning to Booby kindly. "I don't know him myself, but Mr. McAuley vouches for him, and that ought to be enough for us, eh? By the way, just before we dine, would you mind coming into my sitting-room, all of you, there 's something I want to discuss—something that you all want to hear, I 'm sure, something political," he added, lest panic should seize the more guilty of the tribe.

He led the procession upstairs. Melba was waiting in the hall. Jimmy picked him up on the way, and squeezed his hand for courage.

They all filed into Mr. Kirby's private sitting-room, and they found it conveniently large.

As for their host, he began fussing about like a man who is arranging a meeting of directors, and finally took his seat at the head of the large table.

"I think you 'd better sit here, Brassington," he said, pointing to a chair on his right. "And you, Professor Higginson, would you come here?" pointing to a chair upon his left. ".The rest," he added abruptly, "can sit where they like. My lord! it 's beginning to rain!"

They sat awkwardly round him. Mr. Brassington, at least, was used enough to his irrelevancy not to notice the last remark, but Professor Higginson stared. He had had enough to do with mental aberration in the last few days ; he didn't want any more of it.

" It 's beginning to rain," continued Mr. Kirby, turning to Mr. Brassington, " and I 'm sure you didn't bring your Overcoat. It 's May, and you didn't think you 'd want it. Well, I 've taken the liberty of an old friend, and I 've got it here ; it 's hanging up." He jerked his head backwards.

They followed his gesture with their eyes, and sure enough the Green Overcoat was hanging there ponderously and silently upon a peg. It had one will and one purpose, and it had accomplished it : it had found its master.

" You 're a careless fellow, Brassington," said Kirby, hitting that Capitalist rather affectedly upon the shoulder. " Do you know you left your cheque book in the pocket ? "

" Yes," said Mr. Brassington not very pleasantly, " I did."

Mr. Kirby left not a moment for thought.

" Well, gentlemen, I haven't come to talk about that. I 've come to give you some good news. I saw Hogg this morning. You all know Hogg ? He 's the man who handles the dibs at Westminster. He 's a really good fellow, collects stuffed frogs, has hundreds of 'em ! Well, they 've done the straight thing at last, and " (turning to Mr. Brassington) " they 've put you in the Birthday Honours, Brassington ! "

Mr. Brassington jumped.

" It 's a Baronetcy ! "

Then at last Mr. Kirby was silent.

It grew clearer and clearer to Mr. Brassington that

the presence of all these gentlemen round the table was not needed ; but in the course of the next few minutes he had cause to change his mind.

Professor Higginson, as the only elderly man present, thought it was his duty to say, " I congratulate you, sir," to which Brassington answered shortly, " Yes."

Mr. Kirby stroked his chin.

" Professor Higginson," he said pleasantly, " why did you forge that cheque ? "

" *Wha*—" half gasped, half roared the Philosopher, and then he made a great gulping noise with his throat.

The clock on the mantelshelf ticked loudly. Jimmy tried to sit still. Mr. Brassington didn't try to do anything of the sort. He had half risen, when Mr. Kirby with a firm hand pushed him back into his chair.

For a minute nothing was said. Mr. Kirby occupied the minute by tapping slowly at intervals with his fountain pen upon the table. At the end of the interval Professor Higginson saved himself by speech.

He pushed his chair back from him, and stood up as a man does to address the Flap-Doodles at a political meeting.

" Mr. Brassington," he said, ignoring all the others, " it was I who forged your name. I was *imprisoned*, I was tortured, I was constrained by these " (and his voice trembled as he pointed to Jimmy and Melba), " these two young scoundrels, sir, these ——"

" That 'll do, Professor Higginson," said Mr. Kirby, " it 's actionable."

And at that dread wòrd from a lawyer the Professor sat down defeated.

"Kirby," said Mr. Brassington, turning to his friend, addressing him alone, and trying to speak without excitement in a low tone, "I don't understand."

"No, Brassington, you wouldn't," said Kirby kindly, turning as familiarly to him. "You see, Professor Higginson here borrowed your coat."

"He ―― ?" began Mr. Brassington explosively.

"Yes, yes," continued Mr. Kirby, "don't mix up big things with little, that 's what he did—any man would have done it. It was a terrible night, and someone had taken his cape. He just borrowed your coat. It was that night at Perkin's, you remember? The night you were going to Belgium and didn't—ten days ago?"

"Oh, yes, I remember well enough," said Mr. Brassington bitterly.

"Well, there you are," said Mr. Kirby with the utmost simplicity. It 's all quite natural. Just a misunderstanding. Always happening. *They* thought *he* was *you*. Eh? So, why! they just took him off and kidnapped him. That 's all!"

All this explanation Mr. Kirby delivered in the easy tones of the man of the world who is setting things to rights and preventing hysterical people from tearing each other's eyes out.

"There you are," went on Mr. Kirby, flourishing his hands gently in front of him, "there you are! Mr. McAuley couldn't get his money. Thought he 'd got you. Cheque book, no conscious fraud. . . ."

Here Mr. Brassington was no longer to be

controlled. He pushed back his chair, leant over the table, looked at poor Jimmy with a Day of Judgment look, and said with intense determination—

"You shall answer for it, sir, and I will not listen to your father or to your friends."

Mr. Kirby looked up at the ceiling, then he looked straight down the table, then he looked up at Mr. Brassington, and Mr. Brassington sat down.

"Brassington," said Kirby, when he had got his audience, "you have no action against Mr. McAuley, your action is against Professor Higginson. If you bring it, Professor Higginson is ruined, and your son is besmirched, and you look a fool, and the Government has done with you; *and*, Brassington, remember that you owed that money."

"I did nothing of the sort," said the merchant sternly.

"Father," said the wretched Booby, "I'd won more than that off Jimmy, I -had, really! And when I lost back again, unless he'd been paid I don't know what would have happened. I'd have cut my throat, father," said Booby.

He meant it, but it was exceedingly unlikely.

James McAuley for the first time defended his honour.

"Upon my soul, sir, I thought that I was dealing with you, and, good God, if a debt . . ."

Mr. Kirby intervened.

"Be quiet, Mr. McAuley," he said authoritatively, "you are a young man, and I am trying to save you. Brassington," he continued, turning to his friend, and still talking in a strict, authoritative tone, "the money is irrecoverable. Your son had won it, and his winnings had gone in University debts. I

know what they are.   His friend won it back—he
was still a loser, mind—and at once he settled debts
of his own, which he could not bear.   You have
nothing to recover but revenge, and if you take that
revenge you publicly ruin your own son, you make
yourself a laughing stock, you throw away your
future honours and his, and you disgrace a man
of high Academic distinction whom you know
perfectly well to have acted only weakly and foolishly.
You or I might have acted in precisely the same
fashion.   *He* has not had a penny of your money."

"I am the loser," said Mr. Brassington quietly.
"I have lost through ridicule and I have lost
materially—I have lost Two Thousand Pounds."

"The Government," said Mr. Kirby, with a sudden
change of tone to the commonplace, "inform me,
Brassington, that you 've planned a very generous
act.   They inform me—anyhow, Hogg informed me
this morning, or, to be more accurate, I informed
Hogg—that, as the most prominent citizen of
Ormeston, you have put Ten Thousand Pounds at
the disposal of Professor Higginson, whose present
fame throughout the world" (he bowed pleasantly
to the Don, who was fool enough to bow in return)
"I need not—er—dwell upon—you have put Ten
Thousand Pounds, I say, at his disposal for Research
work in the magnificent field of Subliminal Intima-
tions of a Future Life, in which he is at this moment
our chief pioneer."

"I ?" said the bewildered Brassington, catching
the table.   "I promised Professor Higginson Ten
Thousand Pounds for Research Work ?"

"Yes, *you*," said Mr. Kirby firmly; "it 'll be in

the papers to-morrow, and very right the Government were," he continued, " to recognise generosity of that sort by a Baronetcy! Hogg told me he heard it was only a thousand or two, but I gave him the real figures."

" But I never —— " began Mr. Brassington.

" Well, there you are," interrupted Mr. Kirby in a matter-of-fact tone. " They think it, and that 's the important thing. *You*, of course," and here he turned to Professor Higginson, " *you* will never see that money. It isn't there."

" No," said the Professor humbly.

A German in the livery of Cinderella's coachmen solemnly entered the room and told them in broken English that the dinner was served.

Mr. Kirby rose briskly, and they all rose with him.

He went to the Green Overcoat, held it up before him with both hands, and said to Mr. Brassington—

" Now, Brassington, which is it to be ? "

The Merchant, not knowing what he did, slipped into the familiar garment.

How warm was its fur, how ancient its traditional comfort about his person ! What a companion !

" I leave it to you, Kirby," he said in a changed voice. " I 've only to move and I shall do harm all round, and if I sit tight I save eight thousand pounds—and I win."

They were moving to the door, when suddenly Mr. Brassington added—

" Good Heavens ! what am I doing in this coat ? I thought I was going out ! "

" Never mind," said Mr. Kirby, " take it off again. Familiar things remain. They are the only things that do."

And sure enough the bargain held.

* * * * *

Now as to what followed, Reader, or as I hope Readers (for it would be a pity to have only one), I am too tired to tell you much, and there is also an excellent rule that when you 've done telling a story you should tack nothing on.

How the miserable Professor was deluged with begging letters ; how he nearly went mad until Babcock suggested a plan ; how that plan was to pretend that he had left all the Ten Thousand Pounds to the University upon his death and could not touch it ; how his colleagues marvelled that with this new fortune he went on plodding as industriously as ever ; how Sir John Brassington secretly but thoroughly enjoyed his Baronetcy ; how Mr. Kirby delivered three addresses for nothing upon Racial Problems, two in Ormeston and one in the East End of London ; how Professor Higginson was compelled for many years to review the wildest books about spooks, and to lecture until he was as thin as a rail (often for nothing) upon the same subject—all these things you will have to read in some other book, which I most certainly do not mean to write, and which I do not think anybody else will write for you.

How the Guelph University looked when it found there was no Ten Thousand Pounds at all after Professor Higginson's death none of us know, for the old idiot is not yet dead. How they will look does not matter in the least, for the whole boiling of them are only people in a story, and there is an end of them.

THE END